HAUNTED
BLACKPOOL

The author conducting his Blackpool Ghost Walk. (Photo by Peter Taylor)

HAUNTED BLACKPOOL

Stephen Mercer

The
History
Press

*This book is dedicated to the spirits of all those who have helped
to make Blackpool the wonderful town that it is.*

Thank you.

First published 2011

First published 2012

The History Press
The Mill, Brimscombe Port
Stroud, Gloucestershire, GL5 2QG
www.thehistorypress.co.uk

British Library Cataloguing in Publication Data.
A catalogue record for this book is available from the British Library.

ISBN 978 0 7524 6021 5
Typesetting and origination by The History Press
Printed in Great Britain

Contents

	Acknowledgements	6
	Foreword	7
	Introduction	8
one	Blackpool: A Short History	11
two	The Promenade: Trams, Donkeys and Shipwrecks	14
three	North Pier: The Pier and North Pier Theatre	25
four	Blackpool Tower	36
five	Pleasure Beach Resort	42
six	Blackpool Zoo	49
seven	Blackpool's Parks: Stanley Park and Salisbury Woodland Gardens	54
eight	The Winter Gardens: Opera House, Spanish Hall and Empress Ballroom	60
nine	St John's Square	76
ten	The Grand Theatre	80
eleven	Haunted Hotels & Pubs	91
	Sources & Web Links	95

Acknowledgements

THANKS are owed to so many people for making *Haunted Blackpool* possible. To Beth Amphlett, Matilda Richards and all at The History Press for making my dream of writing a book on the 'darker side' of Blackpool a reality, my sincerest thanks.

Thanks to Ian and Julie Lawman for being such good friends and for their encouragement. Long may we continue to investigate the unknown.

To Peter Taylor for attending many ghost tours and providing me with disc after disc of photographs, my grateful thanks. Thanks to Sean Conboy of Photo-Genics for allowing me to reproduce some of his wonderful architectural photography. To Juliette W. Gregson of Blackpool Ghosts Photography, thanks for providing many of your inspirational images for the book.

To Mark, Rob and Jebby (Para-Projects) for being great friends and supporters; thank you.

To everyone who wrote to me, telling me of their encounters with the supernatural; a very special thank you. To name you all would take another book, but without you *Haunted Blackpool* would not be.

Thank you to the managers and staff at many of Blackpool's famous attractions for allowing my ghost tours and investigations to take place.

To Robin Duke and colleagues at the *Blackpool Gazette*; to Ian Shepherd and all the presenters and staff at Radio Wave; to everyone at visitBlackpool and Lancashire and Blackpool Tourist Board (www.visitlancashire.com); thank you all for your support.

To Mum and Dad – thank you for always being there and for simply being you. To Andreas, thank you for your patience and for putting up with me as I pulled my hair out trying to complete this book on time! This book is for you.

Foreword

I have always had a very special link to Blackpool and it is a place I hold dear to my heart. As a child I used to come to the town with my family on holiday. I loved it. Whether I was climbing to the top of the Tower, playing on the beach in good weather or escaping to the amusement arcades in bad, or enjoying a show in one of the theatres and being both scared and exhilarated at the same time when experiencing the rides at the Pleasure Beach.

My link with the town, however, goes much deeper than that. My spirit guide is Charlie Cairoli (1910-1980), who was probably the most famous clown in the country. He spent many years performing at the Tower Circus; perhaps that is why I was drawn to this most famous of seaside towns in my younger years and why I love visiting the resort to this day.

As a psychic medium, I have travelled the length and breadth of the country investigating hundreds of reported hauntings and other experiences of paranormal phenomena – whether whilst working on television shows such as *Most Haunted*, *Famous and Frightened* and *Living with the Dead*, or with ghost hunting and paranormal tour companies. I was particularly delighted when Stephen contacted me a few years ago and asked me to be a guest on his Supernatural Events ghost tours and investigations. I couldn't say no to an invitation to a town I love.

I now count Stephen as a close friend and together we have investigated many Blackpool locations. There are many stories to tell. *Haunted Blackpool* is a collection of some of these stories; not just those ghostly sightings reported in the newspapers, or paranormal encounters written about on websites and social networking sites. These are stories from people who have 'been there' and experienced the paranormal up close and personal.

I am sure you will enjoy (if that is the right word) the stories you will read in *Haunted Blackpool*. Some are funny, some are poignant, and some are just a little bit scary!

Ian Lawman, 2011

Psychic medium and exorcist Ian Lawman.

Introduction

FOR as long as I can remember I have been fascinated by the spirit world and intrigued by all things supernatural. In my teenage years I purchased books on ghosts and haunted buildings, witchcraft, the occult, goodness knows how many decks of tarot cards, rune stones, and much more paranormal and esoteric paraphernalia. As I grew into adulthood nothing changed, except my collection grew larger.

My first encounter with the paranormal occurred when I was a child. I was brought up in a small town in Northern Ireland; opposite my family home were fields that housed cattle, horses and sheep, or were used to grow wheat or hay. Living so close to the countryside was wonderful; I would spend many hours enjoying the exciting world of Mother Nature, taking long walks along muddy lanes, hopping across stepping-stones over streams and rivers. On all my walks I used to stop by one run-down old building. I seemed to be drawn to it every time. Everyone knew this was a haunted house. I had been warned about going into it and told that, if I did, the ghosts who watched over the building would 'get me'!

One evening, I decided to investigate that haunted house and find out for myself if there were any ghosts. I waited until it got dark then put my torch in my pocket, walked across the fields, and found myself at the open doorway to the ruined building. I took a deep breath and ran across the doorstep. I was so nervous I even forgot I had a torch in my hand, and when I did remember to switch it on I had already managed to pass through two rooms. I could see a door in front of me and nervously edged my way towards it. I put my hand out, determined to turn the old-fashioned doorknob. I got within a few inches of it and saw it turn on its own. I couldn't move. I was frozen to the spot. The door started to open towards me. I watched... terrified! The door flung itself wide open, banging against the wall. Then, suddenly, I was thrown backwards. Landing on the floor, I picked myself up and looked around; there was nothing there. I panicked... I ran... I think I even screamed!

So, that was my first experience of the paranormal, but it wasn't my last. Many years later I moved to Blackpool, a town I had visited many times with my family as a child and then on my own as an adult.

Nothing compares to Blackpool's beach with the sun setting over the Irish Sea.
(Photo by Juliette W. Gregson, Blackpool Ghosts Photography)

I finally came to work at Blackpool's Grand Theatre. It was while I was there that I heard stories of the theatre ghost. I would spend many evenings in the theatre, and occasionally I would be one of the last to leave. I would sit in the darkened auditorium hoping to catch a glimpse of something from beyond, or experience some kind of paranormal phenomena. And I did!

I heard footsteps from above the stage when no one was there; I heard banging noises on the stage; I even had my shoulder tapped whilst I was sitting in a seat in the auditorium. In 2006 I started organising ghost tours at the theatre to allow other people to come in and experience what I had.

Over the next few months I spoke to many people about the town. I wanted to find out more about Blackpool's haunted buildings and attractions – I didn't realise there were so many! I was fortunate to be allowed into many of these to investigate the ghostly sightings and sounds that people had reported. I was amazed at some of my experiences and began to operate my company Supernatural Events – ghost tours

Stephen Mercer – author, paranormal investigator and founder of Supernatural Events.

and investigations – in some of the active locations.

Blackpool's history is fascinating, but its haunted heritage is gripping! I hope you will join me on this tour around some of the town's reportedly ghost-inhabited locations and that you find this collection of ghostly tales, as recounted to me by those who have experienced the supernatural, as intriguing and enjoyable to read (and perhaps just a little bit terrifying) as I have had experiencing, researching and writing them.

Happy hauntings!

Stephen Mercer, 2011
www.SupernaturalEvents.co.uk

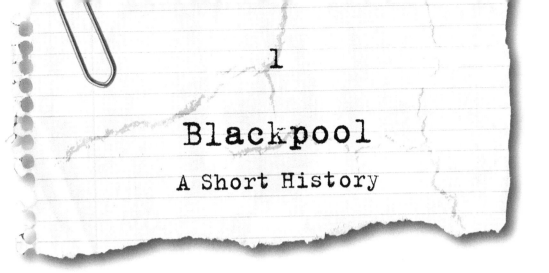

1

Blackpool

A Short History

A very warm welcome to Blackpool, the UK's most famous, most popular, most fun – and most haunted, seaside resort. The town has developed over many years to become the nation's favourite holiday destination. In its youth, Blackpool was a small hamlet situated next to the sea, with much of the surrounding area being marshland. The name of the town originated from the old English name for stream, 'Le Pull'. As the area grew the name became Blackpool, so-called because of the dark-coloured water that found its way via a stream from a small lake at Marton Mere to the sea.

The 1700s saw visitors arriving in Blackpool, many of whom were of the 'wealthier classes', who came especially to bathe in the sea. It was a common belief that the sea held secret cures for illness and disease, and people would travel great distances to dip their toes into the salty waters. Not only did the sea become famous for bathing in, it also became known as the final resting place for many ships that were wrecked in the strong tides and currents along the coast.

Blackpool grew in popularity throughout the late 1700s, when a road was constructed in 1781 through the marshland areas, making the town much more accessible. By the end of the century there were four hotels receiving visitors from around the North West.

The railway arrived in 1840 to the nearby village of Poulton. Six years later the line was extended to Blackpool, allowing even more visitors to travel to the seaside. With the increase in the popularity of the town, more hotels were built to house the ever-growing number of tourists, and entrepreneurs began to build and create attractions to entertain the visitors. Many of the buildings that held these attractions remain to this day; many have stories of ghosts attached to them.

The year 1856 was significant in the history of the town, with gas lighting being installed and the construction of the seafront promenade, which was officially opened in 1870. In 1863 North Pier was opened; it was a promenade pier and a place to enjoy the summer sun. Two further piers followed: Central Pier in 1868, known then

Blackpool – the most famous and most haunted of Great Britain's seaside resorts. (Photo by Juliette W. Gregson, Blackpool Ghosts Photography)

The world's largest mirror ball can be seen on New South Promenade; part of the outdoor exhibition entitled The Great Promenade Show. (Photo by Juliette W. Gregson, Blackpool Ghosts Photography)

as South Jetty, with a theatre, and South Pier with its amusements in 1893. North Pier may have been a place to have gentle fun, but it has had its share of tragedy, from fires breaking out in its theatre to ships crashing into and destroying part of the pier itself.

The late 1800s saw more attractions open to excite the visitors, who were now arriving in their thousands during the summer months. Dr Cocker's Aquarium and Menagerie opened in 1875, followed three years later by the Winter Gardens with its indoor promenade and pavilion. Blackpool became the first town in Britain to have electricity in 1879; the same year saw the introduction of what has become Blackpool's most famous and free attraction, the Illuminations, when eight arc lamps were hung and switched on for the very first time, described as artificial sunshine.

In 1885 Blackpool achieved another first, when it became the first town in the country to have electric trams. In 1890, the largest theatre outside of London – the Opera House – opened. The year 1894 saw the opening of the town's main landmark, Blackpool Tower, followed by the Grand Theatre and the then largest Ferris wheel in the world, the Gigantic Wheel, within the Winter Gardens.

The following century saw the opening of Blackpool's first airport, the opening of the Pleasure Beach, Stanley Park, Louis Tussaud's Waxworks and Blackpool Zoo. The Promenade continued to be developed, and by the 1950s Blackpool had become the most popular holiday destination in the UK. The improved road networks throughout the North West meant that even more people could visit the town. More attractions were built to keep tourists entertained during the 1900s, many of which still stand and are as popular today, including the Sea Life Centre, Model Village, Sandcastle Waterpark and Coral Island Amusements, amongst others.

Blackpool is constantly changing and adapting to meet the needs of its visitors, and to entice more tourists to sample its delights during the holiday seasons. It is still the most popular tourist destination in the UK and, with over 2,000 hotels, guesthouses, B&Bs and caravan parks to accommodate its visitors, it is likely to continue to be so for many years to come.

With phantom trams, haunted theatres, ghost trains with 'real' ghosts, apparitions of donkeys on the sands, the sound of invisible bells ringing, and spectral screams that are said to come from the poor souls who lost their lives in the ships that were wrecked along the coast, it is no surprise that Blackpool has become one of the most popular destinations in the country for another reason – ghost hunting.

2

The Promenade

Trams, Donkeys and Shipwrecks

BLACKPOOL'S famous Promenade, nicknamed the Golden Mile, is full of wonder and excitement. Jutting into the Irish Sea, it is here that you will find many of the resort's legendary attractions, such as Pleasure Beach Resort, Sandcastle Waterpark, Madame Tussaud's, Sea Life Centre, the three piers and, of course, Blackpool Tower, along with amusement arcades, stalls, cafés, novelty shops, trams, open-air artworks – collectively called the Great Promenade Show – and much more.

The Promenade can best be enjoyed on foot along beautiful pathways, green garden areas and the beautiful golden sands of the town's beach, or by bicycle or tram. During autumn, the Promenade becomes awash with colour with the world-famous Blackpool Illuminations.

Trams

Blackpool's trams first appeared in the town in 1885. The tramway is one of the oldest electric tramways in the world and, although the track now runs approximately 11 miles between Blackpool and Fleetwood, it was originally constructed between Dean Street and Cocker Street (between South Pier and northwards past North Pier), a distance of around 2 miles.

With a selection of single and double-deck trams that date back to the 1920s still in operation today, taking a ride on the electric trams are a highlight for many who holiday in Blackpool. There are many variations in the styles of trams including the Standard Car, dating back to the 1920s, the Balloon

Blackpool trams. (Photo by Juliette W. Gregson, Blackpool Ghosts Photography)

The brightly lit and colourful illuminated trams that delight Blackpool's visitors during the Illuminations season. (Photos by Stephen Mercer)

Trams from the mid-1930s, the Coronation Car built during Queen Elizabeth II's coronation year in 1953, the single-deck Rail Cars that had a similar design and look to train coaches in the mid-1950s, and the more modern Jubilee Car dating from the late 1970s and early '80s.

Perhaps the most loved of all, the tram many visitors will queue at the stops to alight, is the Boat Car – a single-deck, open-topped tram so-named because of its ship-like appearance, which came into existence during the 1930s. There have been many other tram designs; many that have sadly come and gone.

During the annual Blackpool Illuminations (in the autumn months of September and October), when visitors flock to the town from all over the world, you can see some of the most decorative and colourful of trams. A selection of single-deck cars were rebuilt in various styles as illuminated and themed trams. Shining bright with colourful lights, you can still see the Illuminated Frigate and the American-style Western Train making their way slowly along the tramway amidst the lights and camera flashes, as people try to capture these marvellous sights.

The Man with the Gas Lamp

The tramway close to the Lytham Road junction with the Promenade is where many have seen the apparition of a man standing in the centre of the tracks, dressed in a smart uniform and holding up a lamp, which he waves from side to side, as if trying to signal to the driver of the tram to stop. Some passengers have seen the man in question and have become worried when the tram doesn't slow down and the driver doesn't seem to notice him. When they look around after the tram has passed by the figure, he has vanished.

George and his father were on a tram heading southwards along the Promenade. It was early evening but already quite dark. They were sitting on the upper deck of an open-topped tram enjoying the ride, feeling exhilarated with the cold wind brushing against their faces.

George could see a figure on the tracks ahead of them and a light swinging from side to side. As they got closer, he could see it was a man dressed in a suit and wearing a cap. He was surprised as it looked like the man was holding a vintage gas lamp. The tram didn't slow down; it just kept going and the man disappeared from view. Worried for the man's safety, George jumped up and ran to the rear of the tram to see where he was, but he had gone. Other people were happily wandering along the Promenade; nobody was shouting or screaming about an accident. He sat down. His father asked him what was wrong, why he had jumped up so suddenly and why he looked so pale. George explained what had happened. His father was surprised; he hadn't seen a thing!

John and his family had just come out of their guesthouse on Lytham Road. They were walking towards the Promenade and planned to go to a fish and chip shop for their evening meal. As they were looking in a shop window, John's youngest son tugged his coat and pointed to a man on the tram tracks who was waving a lamp. They watched as a tram approached and then suddenly the man disappeared. John couldn't explain it.

The illuminated Western Train with the illuminated Blackpool Tower in the background. (Photo by Stephen Mercer)

Maureen and John had come to Blackpool for their honeymoon. Maureen had been visiting Blackpool for many years with her parents and, later, with her girlfriends. She was looking forward to showing John the many wonders of the seaside town as he had never been before.

It was evening when they were on one of the single-deck trams going southwards towards the Pleasure Beach. They had just enjoyed an evening meal and a show at one of the theatres, and were heading back to their hotel. Quite content with their evening out, they were discussing what to do the following day when Maureen stopped talking and pointed in front of her; through the front windscreen of the tram, both she and John could see the figure of someone holding a lamp.

She said to her new husband that it was probably a problem with the track; she had been on a tram before when it had had to be stopped and the passengers were switched to another. She collected her bag and coat, expecting the tram to slowly stop while another was called for to take them on the rest of their journey. However, the tram did not slow down. Maureen and John both looked around them. No one else seemed to be gathering their belongings in readiness to alight. The tram continued.

When it arrived at their stop, John asked the conductor what had happened and who the figure was on the track with the swinging lamp. The conductor laughed. He explained that there had been no one there, but they weren't the first to see a figure with a lamp and that many believe there is a ghost of a man who used to work for the trams many years ago who haunts that part of the tramway.

Tram No. 702

There have been stories for many years of a ghost tram that runs along the Promenade. Darren worked on the Blackpool trams before transferring to buses. He recalls that on countless occasions people have complained about a tram that continues past them even though they are standing at the tram's stop. People see the driver; and many signal to him to stop, but the tram carries on! When asked if they noticed the number of the tram, they all reply 702. Unfortunately, tram No. 702 does not run along Blackpool's tram tracks any more; it was broken down many years ago and, until recently, sat in pieces in the tram sheds.

Mary and Julie were waiting at a tram stop on the Promenade in the North Shore area of Blackpool. They were looking forward to riding the tram to Central Pier, where they were going to see a show. They could see a tram approach from the north and both made ready to board.

Mary thought it strange that the tram wasn't slowing down as it approached them,

so she held out her arm, hoping the driver, who could be seen through the front windscreen, would notice her signalling to him to stop. But the tram continued past. Both women, annoyed that the driver would be so inconsiderate as to leave them stranded at the stop, could only watch in anger as the tram drove further away from them.

The next day, they complained to the conductor of another tram. He asked if they knew the number of the tram. Julie remembered it was 702. The conductor smiled and explained that there was no tram with that number. The ladies were very confused.

David and Mary were walking along the Promenade towards the town. They looked behind them, hoping that a tram would come along that they could hop onto so they wouldn't have to walk any more. They had arrived on holiday from Yorkshire earlier that day and had spent the afternoon and early evening walking along the beach and part of the Promenade; they were tired. At last Mary saw a tram behind them, in the distance. They both hurried towards a tram stop that they could see a little further on. They arrived breathless, but laughing and happy. The tram drew nearer and they looked forward to sitting on their seats and being driven further southwards along the seafront to their hotel.

They waited patiently as the tram drew nearer; but it didn't slow. The tram kept its steady speed and continued past them. They were left open-mouthed, wondering how the driver, who could clearly see them waiting at the stop, could just drive on, leaving them behind. There were lights inside the main carriage and, although there were no passengers, it looked like the tram was in operation. They were so tired that they crossed over the road that ran parallel to the tram tracks and went into one of the larger hotels, where they asked at the bar if they could phone for a taxi.

Over breakfast the next morning, Mary and David discussed the incident with the tram and decided that they would phone the operators and make a complaint. They spoke to the hotel staff member who was serving them breakfast, who said she would ask the receptionist to have the number ready for them when they left the dining room. When they arrived at reception, the gentleman behind the desk asked them what had happened the previous evening. Mary explained. The receptionist asked if they had taken the number of the tram. When David told him it was 702, the receptionist said there would be no point in phoning to complain and told them the tale of No. 702, Blackpool's phantom tram!

Blackpool Donkeys

One of the most entertaining sights on the beach are the herds of donkeys, who carry children on walks up and down the sands. These loveable animals have been part of families' holidays in the resort since the Victorian era and thousands of children have enjoyed the short rides as part of their Blackpool break.

In 1942 the 'Donkey Charter' was set up, which gave details of who could ride the donkeys and stated that the animals must have rest breaks. Many years later, in 2005, Blackpool Council enforced the ruling that the animals could only work forty-eight hours a week, from 10 a.m. to 7 p.m., with a full hour for a lunch break, and that they should not work on Fridays.

The Phantom Donkeys

Some residents and holidaymakers to Blackpool insist that they have seen a small herd of donkeys on the beach close to North Pier on Friday evenings, despite the regulation that they don't work on that day. The sightings have occurred in late evenings during the summer months, and, as the donkeys don't work after 7 p.m., why would they have been seen on the beach?

Robert, his wife Mary and their three children were on a long weekend break from Glasgow; they arrived at their hotel on Friday afternoon and, after quickly unpacking, made their way to the seafront to enjoy some sightseeing. They stopped at one of the ice-cream stalls on the Promenade and, while chatting with their attendant, Robert asked about donkey rides, as he knew the children were excited at the prospect of being carried up and down the beach on them. He was told that Fridays were their day off. Initially disappointed, the family carried on and enjoyed their first day in Blackpool. That evening, they went for a walk along North Pier, the oldest of the town's three piers. After enjoying a ride on the carousel towards the end of the pier, they decided to walk back to the amusement arcade, before returning to their hotel.

It was on their way back that Jenny, the oldest of the three children, shouted with excitement that the donkeys were on the beach. All the family could see them and decided to forgo the arcade in favour of running down onto the beach and riding on the donkeys. Within two or three minutes they had left the pier and were walking down the path to the steps that led onto the beach. When they got to the top of the

Blackpool's famous donkeys.
(Photo by Peter Taylor)

steps they looked to where they had seen the herd from the pier… but the donkeys were gone. They walked onto the beach and looked up and down the long stretch of sand, but there was no sign of the donkeys anywhere. They were left bewildered.

A similar incident happened to Janice and her daughter Isabelle. On holiday from Yorkshire, they were walking along the Promenade enjoying the warmth of the summer sun on a Friday evening when they saw the donkeys on the beach. Deciding to get closer to take some photographs, they descended the steps onto the beach, but, as they got closer, the donkeys seemed to fade away into a mist.

Who, or what, are these phantoms on the sands? Are they memories of donkeys from years gone by?

Pauline and her sons Jack and Ben were about to leave the nearby pier when Pauline heard children's laughter coming from below the pier. Holding onto a railing and looking over onto the sands below, she could see children on donkeys, obviously enjoying themselves, and she joined in with their laughter. Her sons couldn't see the donkeys or hear the laughter; they just thought their mother was playing tricks on them.

When they said they couldn't see or hear anything, Pauline looked at them with surprise. She remembers pointing down to the beach below, where she had seen the children, but they had gone. She walked to the other side of the pier and looked down again. There was no one there.

Blackpool Shipwrecks

It is not common knowledge, but Blackpool and its surrounding area, the Fylde Coast, has become a ship graveyard. Around 130 documented shipwrecks have occurred along this small stretch of coast. Although many of the crews and passengers were saved over the years, sadly there were lives lost.

One of the ships, the brig *The Aristocrat*, crashed opposite what was then known as the Hydro Imperial (now the Barceló Blackpool Imperial Hotel), situated on the north shore area of Blackpool in 1843; it is said that two passengers drowned. In 1848, the *Ocean Monarch*, on a journey from Liverpool to America, sank in the Irish Sea close to Blackpool. It is recorded at the time that 178 lives were lost, though it is believed to be closer to 300. The *Favourite*, another brig, was wrecked, with the loss of ten crew members in 1865. In 1929 the former Fleetwood trawler, *Commandant Bultinck*, was wrecked to the north of Blackpool – three people died.

There are many more records of ships that have become wrecks in the area. The most well-known of these were the *Abana* and the HMS *Foudroyant*.

The *Abana* was a Norwegian ship that was sailing from Liverpool to Florida. Whilst sailing in the Irish Sea in December 1894, she got caught in a severe storm. The crew mistook the recently built Blackpool Tower (which opened that year) for a lighthouse and headed towards it, only to get caught in the strong currents and become wrecked.

The remains of the shipwrecked Abana *can still be seen on a stretch of Blackpool's beach. (Photo by Juliette W. Gregson, Blackpool Ghosts Photography)*

Nelson's former flagship, HMS Foudroyant, fell foul of terrible storms close to Blackpool's North Pier. (Photo courtesy of Local and Family History Centre, Blackpool Central Library)

The crew were saved, as was some of the ship itself; the bell from the *Abana* found a new home hanging in Cleveleys parish church. Some of the wreck can be seen at low tide on the beach near Norbreck, along the north coast of Blackpool.

The HMS *Foudroyant* is perhaps the most celebrated Blackpool shipwreck. The *Foudroyant* was Nelson's flagship from 1798 to 1800. After ending its service, the ship became a tourist attraction, sailing to ports around the world. It was on a tour of the British Isles and was sailing from Southport to Blackpool during early June in 1897 when it anchored at sea between North Pier and Central Pier.

In the early hours of 16 June, Blackpool suffered terrible weather; a storm caused the ship to free from its anchor and it drifted inland. After clipping and damaging the jetty at the end of North Pier, it crashed ashore near Cocker Square, north of the pier. The crew were saved. Some of the ship was broken up to make wooden souvenirs. Much of the ship remained, moored to North Pier, until a further storm in November of the same year laid the ship to rest at the bottom of the Irish Sea.

Boats and Bells

It is said that if you stand at the end of North Pier on a calm evening, you can hear bells ringing. Those who have heard them believe the sounds are made by the crew members who lost their lives on those ill-fated ships.

Best friends Pete and Andy used to fish off the end of North Pier many years ago. They recall sitting all night, waiting for a tug on their fishing lines while enjoying a mug or two of tea under the brightly lit night sky. Andy heard the bells first; it was around 3 a.m. and there was no sound from the sea, and no wind – in fact there no noise at all apart from the bells. Pete heard them shortly after and remembers that the sounds came from out to sea. They looked out with their binoculars, but could see nothing out of the ordinary; there were certainly no boats or ships in view. After just a few minutes, the bells stopped ringing. It wasn't the only time they heard the bells. Andy believes he heard them five or six times in the two-year period that he fished at the end of the pier.

The sinister side of the North Pier. (Photo by Juliette W. Gregson, Blackpool Ghosts Photography)

One of the most frightening stories sounds like it comes from a very popular horror movie. James, another man who regularly fished off the pier, tells of a night when a thick mist drew in over the water and enveloped the entire pier. There was nothing unusual about that; mists and fogs spring up quite often along the seafront of Blackpool. On some occasions you are unable to see more than a few feet in front of you, especially if you are on the pier. What seemed unusual on this occasion, though, were the sounds James could hear coming from the water.

His father was a keen sailor and he was often out on the seas around the North West coast as a youth. He knows the sounds of sails flapping and that is exactly what he heard. What scared him at the time was that the sound seemed to be coming from the water directly in front of him. It was then that he saw a huge shadow looming out of the fog. It was only there for a few seconds but the sounds remained for almost a minute and then all went silent. It unnerved him so much that he decided to leave the fish alone that night and returned home. Could James have seen and heard one of the ghostly schooners that was shipwrecked on the shore nearby many years before?

The Man on the Rocks

The figure of a young man has been seen climbing up the rock-strewn walls from the beach onto the pathway close to Little Bispham, just north of Blackpool, wearing what has been described as rags for clothes, no shoes and dripping wet. He has been seen crossing over the tram tracks and then disappearing into thin air before reaching the main road. Could this young man have been one of the unfortunate victims from the many shipwrecks in the area?

Vicky certainly believes so. Friends Vicky and Katie were staying at a seafront hotel in the North Shore area of Blackpool. After dinner they decided to go for a walk along the pathway by the sea opposite. It was a warm evening and they both felt they needed to walk off the tremendous feast they had just eaten. They crossed the road and tramway and walked onto the path. The sun was just setting and Katie was taking some photographs of the beautiful scene.

Vicky was leaning on the railing at the edge of the path, watching, when she heard the sound of rocks and stones falling nearby. She looked down onto the beach and saw a man scrambling up the rocky wall towards the path. He was about 100 yards away from them. She saw him climb over the wall and it was then that she realised that something was not right. There was a railing along the edge of the path, but the man didn't climb over it, he seemed to go through it. Katie was still taking photographs and didn't see what was happening.

Vicky watched in amazement as the man walked towards the tramway. He was hunched over, soaked through and wearing what she believed to be three-quarter length trousers and a torn, raggedy shirt. As he got closer to the tramway, he suddenly started to fade and then disappeared completely. He hadn't crossed the tram tracks, Vicky was sure of that, but she doesn't know what happened to him. She believes she saw her first ghost.

A number of similar stories have been reported. The ghost has been seen on the beach itself, on the pathway, and climbing the rocky wall. Common to all of these sightings is that he always fades away when he reaches the tramway.

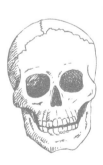

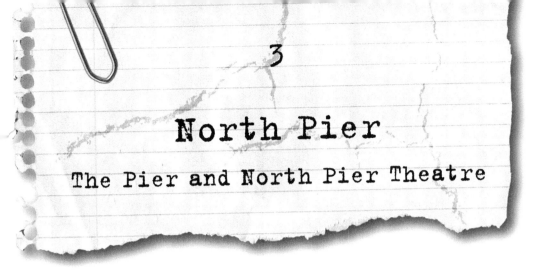

3

North Pier

The Pier and North Pier Theatre

The Pier

North Pier was opened on 21 May 1863 by the Chairman of the Pier Company, Mr F. Preston, with over 20,000 residents and visitors watching the official ceremony from the Promenade. The pier still retains its original Victorian design and magnificence; it is still used today for promenading, and for just sitting and relaxing in the sun.

Within its first year of existence, a landing jetty was added to the pier, and three years later it was extended yet again, to allow the mooring of two pleasure steamers which offered excursions to north Wales, Southport, Liverpool, the Lake District and Isle of Man.

The pier was enlarged in 1874, enabling the building of a restaurant, shops, an Indian Pavilion and a bandstand. Extensions to the pier continued into the early 1900s, when it was widened and electric lighting was installed. A theatre was opened in 1903, along with more shops and an arcade at the pier's entrance. During the 1930s, the bandstand was removed to allow the installation of the Sun Lounge, an area that was shaded from the winds of the Irish Sea but still allowed people to relax and enjoy the warmth of the sun. Changes continued throughout the 1900s, including the addition of the Merrie England bar in 1960 and the two-storey carousel and pier tramway in 1991.

North Pier has suffered much damage over the years. It was struck by a Norwegian ship, the *Sirene*, which got caught up in a storm whilst en route to America in 1892, and was hit again in 1897, when HMS *Foudroyant* was moored to the pier. The Indian Pavilion was destroyed by fire in 1921 and its successor met the same fate in 1938. The current theatre, situated at the end of the pier, opened in 1939.

The Victorian Lady

The phantom figure of a middle-aged lady has been seen sitting on one of the benches close to the pier's entrance/exit. She wears clothing dating from the Victorian era; a long, dark grey skirt that touches the floor, a short jacket fitted around her waist, scarf, gloves, a hat and carries a parasol. She has often been mistaken as a member of staff by visitors, who think she is part of the pier experience – especially as attached to the theatre is the Victorian Tea Room. Nothing could be further from the truth, as some visitors have realised for themselves when they have seen the lady rise from her bench and float along the wooden deck of the pier, before disappearing.

Occasionally the lady has been seen further along the pier, sitting on one of the horses on the lower deck of the Carousel ride, and she has also been seen walking inside the Sun Lounge.

Amanda and Dave were first-time visitors to Blackpool. One of the first places they decided to visit was North Pier, as they wanted to relax after their long coach trip from Aberdeen. They enjoyed a leisurely stroll to the end of the pier, admiring the views out to sea and along the coastline. They had a drink in the Carousel Bar before walking back along the pier to the amusement arcade.

Dave could see a lady in Victorian clothing sitting on one of the benches along the side of the pier, close to the entrance of the arcade and café area. He remembers that as they got closer, she stood up and walked in their direction. As she passed by them, the lady smiled and nodded her head at Dave; he responded with a 'good afternoon'.

Amanda asked him who he was talking to. He replied, 'the lady in Victorian costume who just walked past us,' which confused Amanda, as she had not seen anyone pass by them, especially someone in costume. They both turned around, but the lady was nowhere to be seen.

Blackpool resident Mike was on holiday from work and he and his family decided they would enjoy Blackpool's tourist hotspots. Although they had lived in the town for many years, they had never taken the time to enjoy the town's attractions. Mike, his partner Joanne and their three children were enjoying some leisure time on the pier. They were relaxing in the Sun Lounge when Joanne suggested she take the children on the Carousel ride, while Mike went into the family bar next to the ride to get some more cold drinks.

When he came back out he could see Joanne and their two sons on the ride but their daughter was watching. He went to her and asked why she didn't go on the Carousel. She told him that she did want to go on, but wanted to ride the red horse, and was waiting for the woman in the strange clothes to come off. Mike looked for the woman his daughter described as wearing a long grey skirt, gloves and a funny hat, but he couldn't see her. He thought he might have missed her, and that she and the red horse were on the far side of the ride as it slowed down to come to a halt.

He waited for her to walk around the Carousel, but no woman appeared. Suddenly his daughter jumped up and down with excitement and looked upwards and to her left, laughed and said 'thank you'. When asked what she was doing, she replied that she was saying thank you to the lady for coming off the ride, because she would get to ride on the red horse next.

During the interval of a show at the North Pier Theatre, June and her mother Eileen decided to go outside for some fresh air. They had around fifteen minutes before the second half of the show was to begin, so they went for a quick stroll along part of the pier. They turned towards land and

The oldest of Blackpool's three piers, North Pier, can be seen in the foreground. (Photo courtesy of Local and Family History Centre, Blackpool Central Library)

The haunted North Pier. (Photo by Jebby Robinson, Photo-Genics Para-Projects)

The Victorian Lady has been seen on the bench beneath the lamp. (Photo by Stephen Mercer)

walked past the Carousel ride, sitting down on a bench next to it. There were other people around, walking along the decking or standing chatting and laughing.

June noticed the lady first. She saw a woman in her late forties or early fifties, dressed in what she knew to be Victorian-style clothing, walking towards the Carousel ride. June nudged her mother and told her to look. Eileen saw the peculiarly dressed woman just as she disappeared behind part of the ride. Eileen said to her daughter that she was probably from the show and had sneaked out for a quick cigarette. The two sat for another few minutes before walking back to the theatre. As they passed by the front of the Carousel, they both looked to see if the lady was there; she was. She was on the ride, standing next to a dark-red coloured horse.

What happened next shocked mother and daughter so much that they both went to the theatre's bar for a stiff drink before returning to the auditorium. The lady smiled at them and then stepped down from the ride. As she reached the decking at the pier level, she seemed to shimmer and fade away.

North Pier Theatre

Although North Pier opened in 1863, it wasn't until eleven years later that it housed its first 'theatre', the Indian Pavilion, so-named because of its style of décor. Sadly, the Pavilion suffered at the hands of a fire in 1921; however, it was rebuilt and re-opened, only to be again destroyed by fire in 1938. The present theatre at the end of the pier opened one year later as the North Pier Theatre.

This theatre fell foul of fire in 1985, but was saved from ruin thanks to singer and entertainer Vince Hill, who saw smoke coming from the building when he was leaving the pier after performing in a show that evening and raised the alarm.

There are many stories of the supernatural associated with the North Pier Theatre. A female ghost is said to upset people if they sit in her seat by making banging noises and moving the base of the seat. The spirit of a small dog is said to roam around the front of the seating area close to the stage, the figure of a gentleman is seen walking along the back corridor behind the seating area in the auditorium, and someone – or something – is said to haunt one of the dressing rooms.

Gareth and Stuart investigate haunted locations using scientific methods which included digital and video cameras, audio-recording devices and motion detectors. Using a night vision camera in the auditorium, they were able to track an orb that followed a member of their group. Whilst in the dressing rooms, they asked for noises to be made and were quite shocked when they heard several loud bangs in response. They experienced whispering noises close to a fire exit, which leads out onto the pier from the main auditorium. No explanation for these sounds could be found as the pier was closed to the public; they were the only people on the pier that night inside the theatre.

Don't Sit in My Seat!

Robert, John, Graham and Sarah were at the theatre to see a show when they experienced something they believe to be not of this world. The four friends had just taken their seats before the curtain went up. Robert sat in an end seat next to the aisle; his friends sat next to him and then there were two vacant seats with the remainder of the row being full of other theatregoers.

The friends were looking forward to the show, which was just about to begin, when suddenly the chair Robert was sitting in started to vibrate. There was nothing to cause it and the band had not yet started up. There was absolutely no reason for the vibration to take place.

Robert pointed out to his friends what was going on and asked if they could feel the same in their seats; they all said no. Sarah swapped seats with Robert, and the chair began to shake. She jumped up and moved to one of the empty seats further along the row.

During the interval, Robert moved back to the seat to see if it was still happening; as did Sarah. There was no movement at all. No vibrations and no shaking. Were they being asked to move seats by a spook from the otherworld?

Tina and her husband Greg also had to change their seats while they were watching a show in the theatre. Tina was sitting in an aisle seat; her husband next to her. They had been to see shows there on many occasions and enjoyed the atmosphere of the end-of-the-pier theatre. The concert they had come to see was fantastic and, like most people in the audience, they spent a lot of time on their feet, dancing.

The interior of the North Pier Theatre. Many have seen a ghostly figure wander along the walkway at the rear of the auditorium. (Photo by Stephen Mercer)

After around fifteen minutes of dancing and singing along to the group performing on stage, Greg was a little breathless and decided to sit down. Tina, feeling a little self-conscious dancing on her own, joined him. Within seconds of sitting she felt her seat shake. She thought it was probably caused by her husband tapping his feet in time to the music, or perhaps it was the floor vibrating, caused by others dancing next to them. She looked to her husband; he wasn't tapping his feet. She looked around; there was no one dancing nearby. So why was her seat shaking?

Tina asked Greg if he could feel his seat shake but he couldn't. Their seats were attached to each other, so if one was shaking surely the other would too? Suddenly the shaking became stronger and, at the same time, Tina felt a pressure in the centre of her back, as if someone was pushing their hand against her. She didn't like it and stood up, saying to Greg that they had to move seats. Greg was taken aback by his wife's suggestion.

They had a great view of the stage and if they moved they would have to take seats further back. Tina insisted that Greg sit in her seat to see why she wanted to move. He did, for just a moment, and then he rose from the seat, took his wife's hand and led her to the back of the auditorium, to their new seats!

Greg approached a member of staff as they were leaving the theatre at the end of the performance. He explained what had happened to Tina while she was sat in the seat. The staff member said there had been a few people who had complained about that particular seat. He had heard stories that the seat was haunted by the ghost of a woman who would persuade people to move from the seat if she wished to sit there to watch a show! Had the ghost decided that she wanted to sit in that seat to enjoy the show and didn't want Tina's company?

Blackpool resident Frank was attending his first ghost tour in Blackpool. Earlier that day, he had heard one of the presenters on the local radio station talking about the late-night tour and had made up his mind that he would attend. He had never experienced any kind of paranormal activity, but thought he would go along and see if anything out of the ordinary would happen. If it didn't, he would still get the chance to see behind the scenes in the theatre.

He was talking with the tour guide in the auditorium when he heard a growling noise. Frank thought it sounded like a dog and decided to investigate further. He walked through the seating area to get to the front of the auditorium and stood just in front of the stage. He stayed still and silent, hoping he would hear the growling again. What happened next surprised him.

The Poodle in the Pit

On one occasion, it was noticed that a lady in the front row of the auditorium in the theatre had a small dog, a poodle, sitting in front of her on the floor. The small dog would jump up onto her lap, trying to get her attention and occasionally lick her cheek. Mark and his girlfriend Ann were sat close by and witnessed this take place.

When they saw the lady a little later, they asked her about her dog, as they too were dog owners, but were surprised that her poodle was allowed inside the theatre building. The lady was quite bewildered. She didn't know what they were talking about. She said she did have a dog, but it wasn't a poodle and he wasn't with her that night, he was safely back at home.

The area at the front of the auditorium where the spirit of a dog is often seen. (Photo by Peter Taylor)

He continued to hear the growling noise coming from his left as he stared into the auditorium. He moved quietly in the direction of the sound, and, as he reached the bottom of the steps leading up to the stage, he saw a small white poodle sitting next to the bottom step. It stopped growling as he approached and made a whimpering noise. Frank thought it must have got locked in the theatre and was probably frightened by being somewhere unfamiliar.

Frank put his hand out to the dog, hoping that it would come to him so he could try and calm the poor animal and find out if its owner's name and number were attached to its collar. He was sure someone would be worried. As he held out his hand, the poodle wagged its tail and moved towards him. The dog stopped in front of Frank's hand and licked his outstretched fingers. That's when the dog faded away …

The Spooky Storeroom

Friends Darryl and Danny attended a ghost hunt at the theatre and were investigating the reported paranormal activities that occasionally occur in a storeroom off the auditorium. They made a request for any ghostly presence to make itself known by making noises to communicate with them. They were amazed when they got audible responses.

They asked for a certain number of knocking sounds to be made to prove that there was a spirit in the room with them; the knocking responses were answered correctly. Whilst they were filming this experience with a camcorder, Darryl filmed what many believe to be orbs moving around the small room. Their digital camera lost power rapidly, although it had been fully charged when they began their investigation.

A previous member of the theatre's staff experienced something strange in the storeroom. He was asked to move some chairs that had been used for a concert from the stage to the room. It took him a number of trips to collect all the chairs from the stage, move them down to the auditorium and stack them outside the storeroom.

He took the first stack of chairs and placed them in a corner of the room. He then went back outside the room to collect a second stack. When he went back into the room with the second stack, he found that the first stack, which he had left in the corner, had moved; it was now almost in the centre of the room! He moved the chairs back to the corner and placed a second pile next to them; he then left the room to collect another pile of chairs. When he went back inside, the chairs had been moved again!

He shouted, thinking it might be another member of staff playing tricks on him, to stop moving the chairs. In response to his shouting, he heard several banging noises coming from the corner of the room and then one of the stacks of chairs fell over! He hastily left the room and went to find someone else to complete the job.

Odd Auditorium

At the back of the auditorium is a corridor that leads to the theatre's toilets. It is here, where it is said the ghost of a man wanders.

Alan was in the theatre watching a matinee performance of a summer show, when he left his seat to go to the gents' toilet. As he neared the back of the auditorium, he saw a man walk past the open doorway that led to the corridor that would lead him to the toilets. He turned into the corridor and saw the man in front of him disappearing down the steps that would take him to the gents'.

Alan also descended the steps and opened the door to the lavatories. He expected to see the man, but there was no one to be seen; he was the only person there. What had happened to the man he had just seen in front of him? Where had he gone? There were no other exits… had he seen a ghost?

William and his father John were investigating the reported hauntings of the North Pier Theatre. John had heard about the ghost of a man who walked along the back of the seating area, so he and William decided to spend some time in that area, hoping to see the phantom figure. After spending almost an hour in the area, they decided they had used up more than enough time and would move on to some of the other haunted hotspots within the theatre. As they were about to leave, William saw a shadowy figure pass by them, going in the direction of the toilets.

They decided to follow and began walking down the steps. Just as they reached the door to the lavatories, they heard the sound of footsteps from behind it. There must be someone in there, thought William – perhaps he had mistaken a real person for a

ghostly figure; after all, it was dark! William opened the door and father and son went inside. There was no one there. They checked the stalls; all were empty!

Johanna experienced a number of unexplained phenomena on an investigation at the theatre. She was sitting in the auditorium, just watching what was going on around her. There was a chair close by with its seat in the up position. Others on the investigation had walked past her and the chair on numerous occasions, and it had remained upright. However, out of the blue, it slammed down into its seated position. There was no one near the chair. Johanna was able to take a photograph of the seat in question; when she looked at the image later, it showed an orb directly above the seat. Was it a ghost trying to get her attention because she was perhaps sitting in its seat?

Johanna had other experiences that evening, including the sensation of someone touching her arm – yet there was no one close enough to have been able to physically touch her. She also took a photograph of what she believed to be someone from the group investigating the theatre, sitting quietly in the corner of the auditorium. The photograph revealed an orb close to the ceiling. When Johanna studied the photograph later, she realised that the person in the photograph was not someone from the group at all. Who was it then?

LEFT *Light anomalies (orbs) caught on camera during a ghost tour in the end-of-the-pier theatre. (Photo by Peter Taylor)*

Backstage Scares

Leann was investigating the backstage area of the theatre. She went up some stairs and through a door into a corridor with dressing rooms leading off it. Leann felt a little spooked; she didn't like the feeling of this corridor, but she bravely carried on walking until suddenly, and without warning, she felt she had to leave. She made her way back along the corridor to the door, where she could see other people who were also on the ghost hunt through its glass window. When she went to open the door to join them, she found that the door wouldn't budge, no matter how hard she tried to open it. At the same time, her torch started to flicker and then went out. After what felt like a lifetime, the door finally opened and Leann was able to join the rest of her group.

Disturbances in the Dressing Room

There are stories of a ghost that haunts one of the dressing rooms at the theatre. Pearl, who works as a PR Consultant for the theatre, recalls many performers saying that they have been bothered by a general feeling of unease in the dressing room. They felt that, even though they were alone in the room, they were not alone, and it was sometimes unusually cold, even in the height of summer. She remembers one star asking to be moved to another dressing room, because he believed the room was haunted. Unfortunately, no other cast members were willing to swap with him when they realised why he wanted to change rooms. He finally ended up sharing with the dancers.

Judith's daughter worked at the North Pier Theatre some years ago. While she was there she assisted the late, great British entertainer Danny La Rue to dress. She had just entered his dressing room, and was helping Danny with one of his costumes, when they both heard the door behind her opening and closing. No one had entered the dressing room, and when they looked outside the room, and found nobody else there, they laughed, although a little nervously, saying it must have been the ghost.

Margaret had persuaded her son Ian to go on a ghost investigation in the North Pier Theatre with her. She was a fan of the many ghost-hunting television programmes and wanted to try it for herself. Ian was not as interested, but went along to keep his mother company. After what they experienced that night, Ian wished he had not agreed to go with her.

It was coming to the end of the evening's tour. Margaret believed she had experienced a few paranormal experiences during the event, but Ian had laughed at the idea. He did not believe in ghosts or the paranormal. They decided to spend some time in the star dressing room, as another person on the tour said they had seen a shadowy figure in there. Margaret entered the room first. There were a few pieces of furniture but nothing else. They both sat down; Margaret next to a table and Ian next to the door.

Ian jumped when the door beside him opened slightly and then immediately closed again. He rose from his seat and opened the door, looking out to see if someone had tried to come into the room,

but there was no one outside. He returned to the room and closed the door behind him. No sooner had he taken his seat than the door again opened and closed. He quickly checked outside and again found that nobody was there. He knew that there was no way the door could open and close the way it had without someone physically turning the door handle. He tried to rationalise what had happened, but couldn't.

He stood up and was walking to his mother, who was intrigued by what was happening, when he heard a knock on the door and it opened wide. He could see clearly outside and again saw that they were on their own. How did the door open so wide without someone pushing it? He still cannot understand what happened that evening. Ian has been on many other ghost tours and investigations since experiencing what he now believes to be paranormal phenomena.

Together, Mark, Rob and Jebby make up Para-Projects, a paranormal investigation team who use scientific processes to investigate reported hauntings, hoping to find logical explanations for occurrences that are believed to be supernatural. They investigated the North Pier Theatre along with the nearby Grand Theatre for an episode of their television series *Spook School*. Some of the team, along with the show's director, were in the North Pier Theatre's star dressing room conducting a vigil. Within minutes of being there they experienced an extreme drop in temperature, which they believed to be unusual. As Mark explained, the temperature should have increased due to the body temperature of the people in the room, not decreased.

Mark attempted to radio the rest of the Para-Projects team, who were in another part of the theatre. However, his walkie-talkie failed to function; the power had drained. This was not the only piece of electrical equipment to fail in the room that evening; another team member's camcorder stopped working. Both the walkie-talkie and camcorder had been fitted with new batteries just before the investigation began.

On their way back to the stage area from the dressing room, pinging noises were heard coming from Mark's mobile phone. The sounds were those made when the phone was taking photographs. It had been switched off prior to their investigation commencing, to ensure that it would not interfere with any electrical equipment they were using. At that time, Mark's phone was of the clamshell variety; the only way to switch the phone on would be to open it up and press the power key.

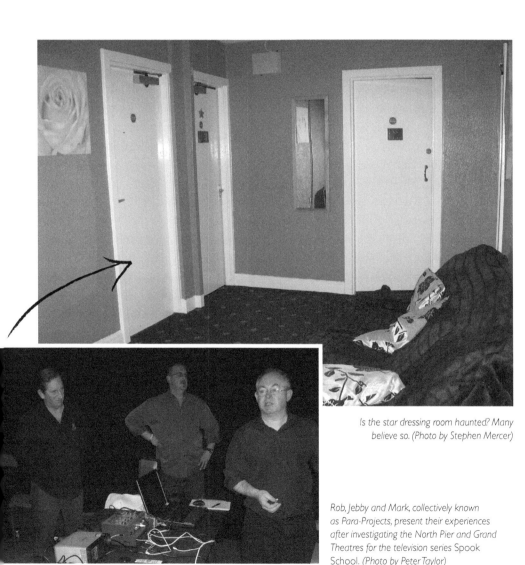

Is the star dressing room haunted? Many believe so. (Photo by Stephen Mercer)

Rob, Jebby and Mark, collectively known as Para-Projects, present their experiences after investigating the North Pier and Grand Theatres for the television series Spook School. (Photo by Peter Taylor)

Blackpool Tower

BLACKPOOL'S pride and joy is, without doubt, the marvellous and imposing Blackpool Tower. Standing at just over 518 feet, the landmark opened on 14 May 1894 after being commissioned by the then Mayor of Blackpool, John Bickerstaffe. He had visited the Great Paris Exhibition five years earlier and was so impressed with the Eiffel Tower that he decided Blackpool should have its own version. The Tower was designed by Manchester-based architects Charles Tuke and James Maxwell, who laid the foundation stone in September 1891, but sadly both passed away before seeing the Tower completed.

The Blackpool Tower Company was formed in early 1891 and construction began almost immediately. Three years later, the Tower was complete and was regarded as the greatest single piece of British engineering of the time. Over 2,500 tons of steel, 90 tons of cast steel and in excess of five million bricks were required to complete the building work.

When Blackpool Tower opened, the cost of entrance was six pence, and if you wanted to go to the top of the tower you were charged an additional six pence. Its attractions included the Aquarium, which survived until 2010, when it was removed to make way for a new Tower Dungeon feature. The fish and creatures living in the Aquarium were given new homes; many were transferred to the nearby Sea Life Centre. Blackpool Tower Circus was a wonderful draw for residents and visitors alike, with its acrobats, clowns and live animal shows (animals stopped appearing in the Tower Circus in 1990). The circus is situated between the four legs of the Tower. During the finalé, the circus ring would be lowered to allow thousands of gallons of water to take its place, and there would be an outstanding display of fountains and lights. The country's most notable clown, Charlie Cairoli, performed at the circus for an amazing thirty-nine years. Near the top of the Tower building was the zoo, which, in later years, was replaced with an indoor garden with waterfalls and fountains. The Tower's original ballroom, the Tower Pavilion, was situated at the front of the complex.

The construction of Blackpool Tower continues in 1893. (Photo courtesy of Local and Family History Centre, Blackpool Central Library)

The world-famous Blackpool Tower having a facelift in 2011. (Photo by Juliette W. Gregson, Blackpool Ghosts Photography)

The stunning Tower Ballroom. (Photo by Sean Conboy, Photo-Genics)

The current Tower Ballroom opened in 1899 and was designed by theatrical architect Frank Matcham, who also designed the original Opera House and the nearby Grand Theatre. It was commissioned by the Tower Company in response to the opening of the Empress Ballroom, within the Winter Gardens complex, in 1896. The mighty Wurlitzer Organ rises majestically from under the stage to entertain those dancing on the beautiful mahogany, walnut and oak flooring. A fire broke out in the ballroom in 1956, partially destroying some of the décor and flooring, but it was restored to its original design, re-opening within a year.

The view from the Tower top is like no other; the breathtaking views across the Lancashire coastline are truly remarkable. Some of the entertainments available to visitors have changed over the years; today there is the Tower Eye with 4D cinema experience, the indoor adventure playground Jungle Jims, the Tower Dungeon, the Tower Circus and, of course, the world-famous Tower Ballroom.

The main area that people have experienced ghostly encounters and other paranormal occurrences is within the Tower Ballroom. There have been sightings of a man's silhouette, believed to walk the length of the first balcony level; a solitary shadow of a lady sitting on the topmost seating area; and an elderly couple on the dance floor.

Intruder from the Other Side

One evening, two staff members were locking up the Tower building. One of the staff was closing up the Ballroom. Whilst crossing the dance floor, he looked up and saw a man walking along the first balcony level behind the back row of seats. He shouted and ran to the stairs. He contacted the other member of staff, telling him to come up quickly as they might have an intruder.

He ran to the stairs and started to climb them. As he reached the first balcony, the other staff member joined him. They could see the silhouette of a man at the far end of the balcony. They ran towards him. As they got closer, they saw the figure walk to the door at the end of the walkway and go through it, disappearing from view. When they reached the door and went to push it open to go after the man, it wouldn't open, it was locked!

Frank and Andrea were seated on the first-floor balcony, watching people dancing in the ballroom beneath them. They were regular visitors to the Tower Ballroom and would usually sit downstairs. However, it was particularly busy that afternoon and there were no seats available. They had had a few dances and decided to have a break, so returned to their seats. Frank thought they could both do with a cold drink and made his way to the staircase, which would bring him back onto the dance floor where the bar was situated.

While Frank was at the bar, Andrea thought she would stroll to the end of the walkway and then return to her seat. As she began her walk, she suddenly felt extremely cold. She returned to her seat, where she put on her shawl to help warm her. She started on her stroll again, along the walkway behind the seats. She had only gone a few feet when she saw a man further along, standing next to the door. He was staring in

The ghost of a man is believed to haunt the balcony level in the Tower Ballroom. (Photo by Peter Taylor)

her direction. As she got closer to the door, she realised that he was still there. She smiled and nodded a friendly greeting to the man, but he didn't return it. Instead he turned around and walked *through* the closed door.

The Lady in the Gallery

Julie and her daughter Lindsey had been on many paranormal investigations but were very excited about attending the first ever ghost tour of the Tower Ballroom. Whilst there, they witnessed something they believe to be truly supernatural.

They had climbed the steps to the top-floor seating gallery and were exploring the area. They were on their own, or so they believed. As they were approaching the seats in the gallery, Julie thought she could see someone sitting close to the front of the balcony, looking down onto the dance floor below. She told her daughter what she could see and asked her to look. As Lindsey looked, she let out a small scream. The person in the seat slowly faded away before her eyes.

They were just calming down when a woman who was also on the tour came to ask if they had seen someone sitting in a

The Tower Ballroom gallery seating, where the silhouette of a ghostly lady has been seen. (Photo by Peter Taylor)

The seating around the beautiful Tower Ballroom, where the apparition of an elderly couple has been seen by both dancers and spectators. (Photo by Stephen Mercer)

seat close by them. She had seen the lady too from across the ballroom, on the other side of the balcony.

Ghostly Ballroom Dancers

The shades of an elderly couple have been seen sitting at a table on the ground floor of the ballroom. They sit for some time, silently taking in the view of those dancing on the floor, and enjoying the music played from the stage. The couple get up and the gentleman leads the lady onto the floor. They begin to dance and, as they start to spin, they also fade away.

Jimmy and Joyce, regular dancers at the Tower Ballroom, believe they saw the couple sitting at the table next to them. They had just left the dance floor and returned to their table, when they saw an elderly lady and gentleman seated at the next table along. They said hello to the couple; their greeting was returned with a smile and a nod. They sat down to relax before their next dance and noticed their neighbours stand up, walk onto the floor, and join in with other dancers. Joyce continued to watch them and, right before her eyes, saw the couple disappear into thin air.

Laura was a student who worked at Blackpool Tower during her summer break from university. She spent most of her time in the ballroom, helping the bar staff and collecting empty glasses left on tables. She had heard that the Tower Ballroom was haunted and, as she was fascinated by all things eerie, she hoped she would see something that she could not explain rationally. And see something she did.

One afternoon, when she was collecting empty glasses and rubbish that had been left behind by visitors to the famous ballroom, Laura was making her way back to the bar when she saw an elderly couple sitting at one of the tables. She recognised them; they had sat in the same seats at the same table for the last three days in a row. As Laura neared the table, she said hello and asked if they were enjoying themselves. The elderly gentleman replied that they were having a jolly good time watching so many people dance.

Laura thought it would be polite to offer them a beverage. She would bring whatever they chose to them so that they didn't have to go to the bar. The lady thanked her and asked if they could have two teas. Laura said she would be back with the drinks shortly. She collected the teas from the bar and began her short walk to where the elderly couple were seated. She could see them through the crowds of dancers, still at the same table.

As Laura got closer, the couple rose from their seats and made their way onto the dance floor. Laura placed the teas on the table and watched as the couple began to dance, mingling with the other couples on the floor. As she watched, the elderly couple slowly faded away. Had Laura seen two ghosts? She thinks so.

5

Pleasure Beach Resort

THE Pleasure Beach was founded by Alderman William George Bean in 1896, who bought the forty-two acre site on which the park now stands. Rides were introduced gradually, including the ever-popular Sir Hiram Maxim Flying Machines, the River Caves of the World, the Water Chute, Toboggan Slide and the Joy Wheel.

The First World War halted any plans to expand and add new rides; however, during the 1920s and '30s, new excitements built included the Dodgems, a boating pool, the Big Dipper, the Ghost Train, Fun House, Grand National and the Pleasure Beach Express. The Ice Dome was also opened during the 1930s.

During the Second World War, Blackpool was still very much open for business, and thousands of military personnel and evacuees were able to forget a little of their troubles by enjoying the entertainment in the town, especially all the fun of the fair at the Pleasure Beach. Exciting rides continued to be added to the park, including the Haunted Swing and Derby Racers during the 1950s, and Alice in Wonderland and the Astro Swirl in the 1960s.

During the 1990s, the exterior of the Pleasure Beach was re-designed to include an Edwardian-style shopping complex, Ocean Boulevard, along the Promenade. Also in this decade, Europe's fastest and tallest rollercoaster, the Pepsi Max Big One, was added, along with Trauma Towers and Ice Blast. A new cabaret and hospitality venue, the Paradise Room, opened in 1995.

The new millennium saw the opening of Valhalla, and in years to follow Spin Doctor, Bling and Infusion. In 2003 Pleasure Beach opened its own hotel, The Big Blue. The year 2011 saw a collaboration with Nickelodeon to transform part of Pleasure Beach into Nickelodeon Land. New rides were added and some re-themed, including SpongeBob's Splash Bash, Avatar Airbender and the Rugrats Lost River.

Sadly, the park has suffered a number of fires over the years, which have damaged or destroyed some of its rides, including the Fun House in 1991, and Alice in Wonderland and Trauma Towers in 2004.

Today, the re-named Pleasure Beach Resort is home to more than 140 rides and attractions, restaurants, cafés, shops and

breathtaking shows, such as the Hot Ice and Beyond Belief. It is no wonder that the park is the country's number one tourist attraction.

The Ghost Train

The park attracts not just the living, but apparently the dead as well. Many ghosts are said to haunt Pleasure Beach Resort; none more so than the spirit of a former ride operator who haunts the Ghost Train. Cloggy, so-named because of his choice in footwear, likes to wander through the ride. His heavy footsteps have been heard clanking against the train's tracks by staff late at night, after the ride has been shut down. On several occasions, he has even shown himself as a faint spectral form.

Cloggy

John used to work at Pleasure Beach Resort some years ago. He had heard the rumours of the phantom that haunted the Ghost Train and wanted to see if there was any truth to the stories. One night, after all the rides had been shut down and visitors to the park had left, he and two other staff members stayed behind. It was dark as they made their way to the Ghost Train; it made John, who was already nervous about his adventure, even more uneasy.

The three colleagues stood in front of the ride, trying to persuade each other to walk closer to the entrance. Together, they edged their way towards the tracks. As they reached the queuing platform, they stopped abruptly. John heard what sounded like footsteps walking to their right, close

The famous Ghost Train at Pleasure Beach Resort, said to be the haunted home of 'Cloggy'. (Photo by Stephen Mercer)

This photograph was taken on a ghost walk through the Ghost Train in the dead of night. Could the light anomaly (or orb) caught on the image be Cloggy making his way along the tracks? (Photo by Peter Taylor)

to the operator's box. He shouted out, asking if anyone was there, but received no reply. The footsteps became louder. All three workmates could hear them now. They made a hasty retreat away from the platform – but not before John saw a mist surround the bottom of the operator's box!

Members of the public have reported being touched or tapped on their shoulders or back when they have been travelling through the darkly lit tunnels. There are effects, of course, which are used to make the experience a scary one; however, there is no explanation as to why people feel they are being touched. Could it be Cloggy making his presence known? Many think so...

Robert finally persuaded his wife Jenny to go on the ride with him. They had spent the afternoon on some of the white-knuckle rides and, although they had been to the park many times before, they had never taken a trip on the Ghost Train. Jenny really didn't want to go, but finally, after much persuasion, she relented and queued at the gate with her husband. They got into their carriage ready for the fun to begin. Fun was not the word that Robert and Jenny now use to describe their venture into the Ghost Train.

Their journey started well. They laughed and screamed, enjoying the thrill of the ride. They got to one point where their carriage went through a door and round a bend. Although it was dimly lit in that part of the tunnel, Jenny could see a figure ahead of her. Lights started to flash on and off and electronic screams started up. She could see the figure much more clearly now. It was a man. For just a second she thought it looked like he was walking towards them. He looked extremely ominous and very lifelike. Jenny was expecting the figure to be pulled upwards or sideways away from the tracks as they got closer, or thought that their carriage would turn another bend before it reached him. But the figure of the man didn't move, nor did the carriage turn a bend; instead, it continued straight ahead and, just before they ran into the mysterious man, he faded away. When Jenny and Robert alighted from their carriage, Robert commented how pale she looked; he teased her and laughed. She scolded him, saying that it was scarier than she had expected, especially the bit where the frightening figure of a man faded away just before they almost crashed into him. Robert didn't know what she was talking about. He hadn't seen a man in front of them. He hadn't seen anyone. Had Jenny seen the ghost of Cloggy?

Ian Shepherd, a presenter on Blackpool's local station Radio Wave, attended the first ever ghost tour of the Pleasure Beach, which included an investigation inside the Ghost Train. He was with a small group of people when they heard clomping sounds. He asked those beside him to remain quiet. The sounds continued. They came from further ahead, on the tracks.

One of the group members, Sam, decided that she would check to see if there was anyone there. She walked hesitantly, with her flashlight shining in front of her. She rounded the bend and disappeared out of view of the others. Ian could still hear the noises and was worried about Sam; he started to walk forward when he heard a scream and then Sam came into view. She was terrified. She believes she saw the now infamous Cloggy appear just in front of her, after walking through a wall!

Radio presenter Ian Shepherd on the hunt for Cloggy. (Photo by Stephen Mercer)

Ian persuaded Sam to go with him so they could investigate further. It wasn't long before they returned to the group – after hearing stomping noises coming from above them, and a screeching noise beside them. Was it Cloggy trying to scare them? If it was, he certainly succeeded.

The Arena

The Arena at Pleasure Beach Resort is the home of the spectacular Hot Ice show, a dazzling display of ice skating from some of the world's top skating champions. But the stars of the show skimming along the ice, dancing to amazing choreography and performing breathtaking aerial work, are not the only thrills to be experienced at the Arena. There have been several reports of hauntings taking place here, including a single spectral skater seen dancing on the ice late at night; an elderly woman in one of the rooms above the stage; and several people running down the steps of the seating area, who make their way onto the ice.

The Spectral Skater

Bobby, one of the managers at the Arena, was doing his rounds late one evening, ensuring that there was no one left in the building before it was locked up for the night. He walked through the building, ensuring doors were closed, corridors were clear and tidy, and finally he made his way towards one of entrances to the seating area, to look around the Arena's vast auditorium. As he drew closer to the stairs, he saw the figure of a man in front of him. He raced after the figure and, when he looked towards the stage, he saw the man on the rink itself. He was dressed in a white shirt and black trousers, and he was simply skating around on the ice. He would not have looked out of place during the day; however, it was late evening and the Arena was closed. There was no show taking place; there were no skating classes that evening; there should have been no one in the building apart from Bobby. He called out to the man, but was ignored. He walked down the aisle steps until he reached the barrier between the seats and the ice, and called again. The man did not respond and carried on skating around the rink.

Bobby decided to call out again and, if the man did not stop and respond, he would send for security. He shouted loudly to the man to stop. He could hear his words echo around the Arena. The man stopped in front of the stage and turned to face Bobby. That was when he disappeared.

The stairs where Bobby first saw the spectre
of an ice skater. (Photo by Peter Taylor)

The seating bank where the ghosts of the Arena have been seen before running down onto the ice. (Photo by Peter Taylor)

'Get Out of My Room!'

Radio presenter Ian also experienced something he cannot explain when the ghost tour he was attending moved into the Arena. The group he was with that evening were on the ice stage, and also in various rooms to the side of the stage and above it. He was talking with the manager, Bobby, about some of the ghostly stories that people have reported about one of the rooms above the stage, when he suddenly felt an overwhelming sense of sadness. He couldn't explain it and had to be led out of the room. A little later, Ian returned to the room to see if he would have the same experience. However, on his second visit he was fine.

The room is said to be haunted by the presence of an elderly lady. There have been reports from both staff and performers that, when entering the room, they have seen the lady, who has asked what they are doing there and said, 'Get out of my room!' The door would often close on its own accord once they had exited the room.

Onto the Ice

Claire and Mike run a guesthouse in Blackpool and were having a rare evening out. After a meal and a walk on the Promenade, they enjoyed a performance of the Hot Ice show. As the show ended they, like everyone else in the Arena, were on their feet clapping and cheering. It was then that Mike saw something strange.

As they looked at the stage, Mike could see around ten people running down the stairs and climb over the barrier onto the ice. As their feet touched the ice, they seemed to be enveloped in a mist and disappeared from view. Mike thought he was going mad, and when Claire said that she hadn't seen anyone run down the steps or climb over the barrier, he decided he was definitely mad. Or was he?

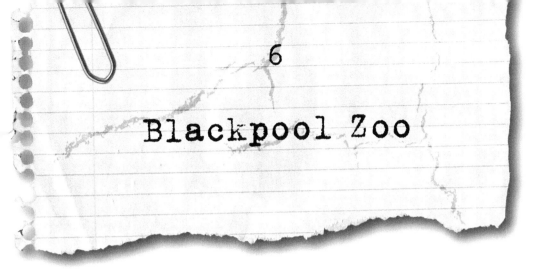

Blackpool Zoo

THE site on which Blackpool Zoo stands has an interesting history. The Blackpool Municipal Airport was officially opened on this site in 1931 by Prime Minister Ramsay MacDonald. However, when the Second World War broke out on 3 September 1939, the airport was requisitioned by the RAF as a parachute training centre. It was re-named Stanley Park Aerodrome. Additional hangars were built to give undercover space where Wellington Bombers were assembled and then flown off to other RAF sites.

When the war ended in 1945, the RAF relinquished its ownership of the airport; however, aircraft was never flown from the site again due to another airport at Squires Gate becoming more suitable for flying in and out of the town. The Stanley Park site was taken over by the Blackpool Borough Council and used as one of its main storage resources. Between 1953 and 1972, the site became the home of England's oldest agricultural show, the Royal Lancashire Show.

In 1969 Blackpool Tower Zoo closed its doors, but the council was adamant that the town should have a zoo. A proposal had been put forward in 1962 for the Stanley Park site to become zoological gardens, but it wasn't until 1969 that the plans were drawn up. Other suggestions for the site included a Formula One racing circuit, a racecourse, a speedway, and even Disney was mentioned – but this option faced fierce opposition from many of the local attractions.

The zoo proposal was accepted and, on 6 July 1972, Blackpool Zoo was opened by Johnny Morris, presenter of television show *Animal Magic*, who arrived at the zoo astride an elephant, accompanied by Blackpool's Mayor in a Rolls-Royce. Over the years the zoo has expanded, with many changes on site. Its offices and education classroom were situated in the original air traffic control tower building, and several hangars used to build aircraft became home to animals – such as the current elephant house – and were used for storage of food and maintenance equipment.

There have been reports of a ghostly gentleman who wanders around the elephant house, where strange noises have been heard and things have moved on their own. There

Blackpool Zoo – it isn't just the animals that you might hear shriek! (Photo by Charlie Headley Photography Ltd)

are also accounts of a spirit presence that can become quite mischievous in one of the hangars that is used as storage for the zoo.

The Hooded Man

Amanda was walking the short distance between Stanley Park and Blackpool Zoo to attend a ghost investigation. She and her friend Sarah were walking along the footpath next to Salisbury Woodland Gardens and could see someone ahead of them, walking in their direction. They thought it must be someone from the zoo who had finished work and was walking towards the main road.

Amanda realised, as he got closer to them, that the man was wearing a dark robe that seemed to be tied in around his waist. He looked like a monk with a hood over his head. He was walking with a large stick. Both Amanda and Sarah stopped and watched as the man began to walk down a pathway leading into the gardens at the end closest to the zoo entrance. He faded away before he reached the bottom.

The man in the robe has been seen on another occasion; this time inside Blackpool Zoo. Vanessa was inside one of the large hangars, exploring and taking photographs. Later, at home, she was viewing the photographs on her computer and realised that one image showed the figure of a man wearing a black robe with a hood. His face was partially covered by both the hood and his hand, but she could see that he looked as though he was laughing. She knew there was no one in the hangar wearing a hooded robe at the time she was taking the photographs. Could this be the same hooded man seen by Amanda and Sarah?

The Elephant House

Lynne is a keen photographer and regular visitor to Blackpool Zoo, and has experienced supernatural phenomena there on a number of occasions. On one occasion, she was in the Elephant House and sensed that there was a person behind her. Lynne stopped what she was doing and turned around to talk to whoever was there; however, there was no one to be seen.

Mark also experienced the same feeling in the same area. He was watching the elephants and one was quite close to him. The elephant turned and looked in his direction and, at the same time, he felt that someone had just walked behind him. He looked around and saw a gentleman walking away from him; the man stopped, turned, and stared directly at Mark, before disappearing into thin air. When asked to describe the gentleman, Mark said he was wearing a boiler suit and had very short hair; could this have been the apparition of an RAF airman, or someone who worked there during the time the site was the Stanley Park Aerodrome?

*The Elephant House –
believed to be one of
Blackpool Zoo's most
haunted locations.
(Photo by Peter Taylor)*

*An orb shines bright in the
elephant enclosure – is this
the spirit of the man Andrew
saw? (Photo by Peter Taylor)*

Marie and her nine-year-old son Andrew were enjoying a day out at Blackpool Zoo and ventured into the Elephant House to see the animals. Andrew had his colouring pencils and paper with him and sat down on his bag to draw a picture of one of the elephants for his mother. When he had finished, he stood up. His mother watched as he held the picture out in front of him towards the elephant enclosure, smiled and giggled. Marie asked what he was doing. Andrew said he was showing his picture to the zoo man, who said it was a lovely likeness to the elephant. When she asked her son where the man was, he said he had been standing next to the elephant but, after he was shown the drawing, he vanished. Marie couldn't see anyone inside the enclosure.

On a ghost hunt held at the zoo, Graham and his family were investigating a non-public area in the elephant house. They were in a room that was utilised as both office space and a storage room. They had been calling out, hoping to get some sort of response… and they did. They heard a metallic noise from ahead of them. They shone their torches in the direction of the sound; against the wall opposite them was a filing cabinet and, as they watched, a drawer opened on its own. They fled the room.

Zoe and her friends were visiting the zoo for the first time. She wandered off to watch one of the elephants in the enclosure eating. She was amazed at the size of the creature; she had never been so close to one before. While she was studying the elephant, she saw a member of the zoo staff walking across the enclosure and stopping a few feet from the railings. He was looking around as if he was searching for someone. He then started to walk in her direction.

When he approached the railings she said hello. He didn't respond, and seemed to stare right through her. She felt a chill on the back of her neck and shivered involuntarily. The man turned away from her and walked back towards the centre of the enclosure. The man then appeared to disintegrate and Zoe saw a mist in his place. He had completely disappeared.

When asked to describe the man by her friends, she said he was tall and wearing a boiler suit. Could this be the same ghostly apparition that Andrew described to his mother? Was it the ghost of the elephant house?

The Horrible Hangar

Psychic medium and exorcist Ian Lawman visited Blackpool Zoo to lead an investigation into some of the reports of paranormal activity there. He was in one of the original aerodrome hangars, which is now used for storage, with a group of people. He sensed that there was a presence in a small room off the hangar and went with some of the other paranormal investigators to check it out.

Within a few minutes, screams from some of those in the room were heard. John was there. He describes the room as being small, dark and cold; the only objects present were some plastic crates that had been stacked up in one corner. There was no one near these; everyone was huddled together in the opposite corner. Suddenly, noises started to come from the corner where the crates were piled up. As the members of the group looked in that direction, the crates fell, crashing to the floor. John is sure they were pushed over by an unseen force.

On a ghost tour at Blackpool Zoo, Simon experienced the paranormal up close and personal. He was investigating some of the smaller rooms off the main hangar. He was working with a crystal pendulum in the hope that it would move in various directions to indicate answers to the questions he was asking. It was the first time he had used this method to contact a ghost or spirit being.

In the main hangar there was no movement from the pendulum. He tried some of the smaller rooms; again no response. It was almost time to leave the hangar when Simon went into one final small, dark room. As soon as he asked if there was a ghost with him, the pendulum started to spin quite aggressively. He excitedly began asking more questions but the answers made no sense. Simon heard the group being called back together; it was obviously the end of the investigation and they would return to the main zoo buildings before returning to their homes. He decided to say goodnight to whatever ghost was nearby.

That was when he felt a pressure on the centre of his back, as if someone was pushing him. The force was extremely powerful and he stumbled forward because of it. The pendulum was pulled out of his hand, landing almost 4 feet away from where he stood. Simon ran out of the room to find one of the hosts for that evening. He explained what had happened and asked if someone else would go in to retrieve the pendulum, as he refused to step foot in the room again. The incident had frightened him too much!

7

Blackpool's Parks

Stanley Park and Salisbury Woodland Gardens

Stanley Park

The beautiful Stanley Park is situated just ten minutes' drive from the centre of Blackpool and only a few minutes' walk from Blackpool Zoo. The land was acquired during the 1920s, for the purpose of building parkland. The local council commissioned architects T.H. Mawson & Sons to design what was to become one of the region's finest and most inspiring parks. Stanley Park was officially opened and unveiled to the local population in 1926 by the 17th Earl of Derby and Sir George Edward Villiers Stanley, in whose honour the park was named.

Within the grounds of Stanley Park are found the beautiful Rose and Italian Gardens, numerous water fountains, the bandstand, conservatories, Cocker Clock, the Art Deco-style restaurant, bowling greens, and ornamental bridges crossing over the impressive boating lake. If you want to relax and while away the hours surrounded by Mother Nature, this is the place to go... by daylight that is!

As the light of day fades, some areas of the park can take on a more ominous feel.

In one area, close to the edge of the boating lake, there is a small copse, dense with ancient trees and shrubbery. It is here that some have seen the shadowy figures of an elderly couple, sometimes sitting on a bench or walking along the winding paths towards one of the bridges that cross the lake.

A Couple of Ghosts

Angela, a local resident who once lived close to the park, has seen the figures on a number of occasions. She and her boyfriend, John, used to go jogging inside the grounds of the park in the early evening hours after they finished work. It was during one of their runs that she first saw the couple. She and John had just entered the park close to the lake and had decided to run first around the wooded area and then carry on into the more open land close to the bandstand. Just moments into their jog, Angela saw an elderly couple walking along the path towards them. She started to jog up on the grassy verge to the

The pride of Blackpool – Stanley Park. (Photo by Stephen Mercer)

The beauty of the water features and flower gardens are breathtaking. (Photo by Stephen Mercer)

The path in the park where the spirits of an elderly couple have been seen by joggers. (Photo by Stephen Mercer)

The bench where William and his father saw the shadowy figures of an elderly couple. (Photo by Stephen Mercer)

side of the path to allow the couple to carry on walking without being disturbed.

As she got closer to them, she smiled and said 'Good evening' as she passed. She thought it rude that her usually friendly boyfriend had ignored them and turned around to scold him. He had stopped and was staring at her with a look of bemusement on his face. He asked who she was saying hello to and why she was running on the grass. She explained why she had moved off the path and how she thought he was rude not to say hello to the couple that had just walked past them. When John said he hadn't seen anyone – and he was right behind her – she thought she was going a bit crazy. She laughed it off and carried on running, trying to figure out what had just happened.

Just a few weeks later, Angela and John were back in the same area. She saw the same couple sitting on a bench at the far end of the lake. She stopped to point them out to John. When she looked back again to where they were sitting, they had gone. She decided to run around that part of the park to catch up with them, just to prove to her boyfriend that she wasn't seeing things. She never caught up with them then, and to this day hasn't either.

In the same wooded area by the lake, fishing is permitted. Anthony, an experienced fisherman, would regularly take his son, William, to the park to teach him the art of fishing. They both enjoyed the park and would stay a few hours on each visit. After spending time endeavouring to make a catch, they would walk to other parts of the park, enjoying the smells of the trees, the fresh air, and their packed lunch by the lake.

On one occasion, Anthony heard his son talking to someone; he thought nothing of this, as his son would talk to others fishing nearby and always said hello to families passing by; his son was a very polite young man. It wasn't until he heard lots of laughter that he turned around. His son was sitting on the nearby bench, still holding one of his sandwiches, and laughing. He asked William who he had been talking and laughing with; he was told that it was an old man and woman. When the father asked his son where they had gone, his son pointed to the path just a few feet away and said they were just there. William waved and shouted goodbye as his father looked in the direction his son was waving, and saw two shadowy figures disappear into thin air.

June enjoys taking her cocker spaniel George for walks in Stanley Park. She has seen what she describes as two phantom figures, as well as hearing strange laughter.

On three separate occasions close to the boating lake, George has simply stopped and sat down, staring at one of the benches nearby. When she tries to coax him to move on, he throws his head in the air and howls! She has to drag him away and, as he finally moves, she hears what sounds like the cackling laughter of an old lady. Twice she has looked around quickly when safely past the bench, and has seen what appears to be the shadowy figures of two seated people. She doesn't tend to stay in this area of the park for long.

Salisbury Woodland Gardens

Close to Stanley Park, and situated next to Stanley Park's Golf Course on the driveway to Blackpool Zoo, is the smaller Salisbury Woodland Gardens. The Gardens were planted back in the 1930s, and in 1993 the place was designated a County Biological Heritage Site for its flora, which includes lichens, fungi and moss. The wonderful Gardens are a testimony to those who care for and nurture the many exotic species of trees and plant life that grow there.

The Gardens are criss-crossed with tree-lined pathways which wind their way through shrubs and plants, with a wooden bridge over a meandering stream. In every area of the Gardens you can hear the sounds of birds high in the trees and the hum of insects buzzing all around. The wildlife found in Salisbury Woodland Gardens is amazing; you may see kingfishers near the stream and woodpeckers on the branches of some of the trees. You might hear the bustling of squirrels in the shrubbery and, if you visit the Gardens after dark, you might be fortunate enough to see some of the small, brown insect-eating bats that live there.

The entranceway to Salisbury Woodland Gardens. (Photo by Stephen Mercer)

The Man in the Uniform

Many who have visited Salisbury Woodland Gardens have commented that they have seen uniformed RAF soldiers from the Second World War era wandering around the area. This is not as surprising as it may seem, however, as Blackpool's Municipal Airport was situated on the site that is now Blackpool Zoo, next to the Gardens, and when the Second World War broke out was requisitioned by the RAF and became an integral part of the war effort. Could the figures seen in the Gardens be ghostly figures from the past?

Alison and two of her work colleagues were attending an overnight ghost hunt at the nearby Blackpool Zoo and decided that they would walk through the Gardens on their way to the zoo's entrance. She knew nothing of the area and did not know of the existence of Salisbury Woodland Gardens. It was starting to go dark as the three friends entered the Gardens and, though they could see the lit footpath and road leading to the zoo, they were all a little bit nervous but at the same time quite excited.

As they walked along the path they heard whispering. At first they thought it was the wind rustling the trees, but when they shone torches at the branches above their heads there was no movement. They walked further on and heard the whispering again. They could see a light in front of them and thought it might have been someone going on the same ghost hunt as they were and so they called out. There was no answer. They walked towards the light and, as they did, the whispering grew louder. They called out once more and, yet again, there was no response.

They decided to go a little further into the Gardens before walking up one of the trails onto the main footpath that they could see to their right. As they walked, the whispering voices became louder and suddenly they saw the figure of a man in uniform walk across their path. They couldn't make out exactly what type of uniform he was wearing, but Alison was sure it was an 'old-fashioned' uniform.

Light seemed to emanate from the figure and, as he walked past, the man looked directly at them before walking into the trunk of a tree and disappearing.

Joan, a student, would often go into Salisbury Woodland Gardens. She was researching the plant life in the Gardens for a botany project at university. She remembers walking over the wooden bridge and then making her way along one of the paths towards the far end of the wooded area, stopping by the stream.

She was kneeling to take close-up photographs and samples of the foliage around her to study later, when she heard a horrible screeching sound. She was instantly worried and frightened, as the noise originated behind her. She turned around and saw the figure of a man running further down the path, away from her. She heard the screech again and the man vanished. She later described him as wearing what looked like a blue suit with a belt around the jacket, and wearing a hat. Could this have been the same airman that Alison and her friends have seen?

An airman isn't the only ghostly figure to have been seen in the Gardens. Other reports include the sighting of a monk, or cloaked man, walking slowly along the pathways with the aid of a staff and carrying a burning torch.

The path in Salisbury Woodland Gardens where visitors have encountered the shade of a man in uniform. (Photo by Stephen Mercer)

8

The Winter Gardens

Opera House, Spanish Hall and Empress Ballroom

OPENED on 11 July 1878, the Winter Gardens complex was to be a series of promenades, conservatories, gardens, theatres, an indoor skating rink and concert rooms, designed to attract Blackpool residents and visitors. Incorporated within the Gardens is the Pavilion Theatre; a small, intimate theatre that became one of the town's premier music hall and variety theatres and during the 1930s it showed the exciting 'talkies' – movies with sound! The British Raj-inspired Indian Lounge, which later became the Arena, and the impressive Empress Ballroom, with its 12,500 square feet of dance space, both opened in 1896.

The current Opera House, situated within the complex, is actually the third incarnation of this impressive theatre. The first was designed by famous theatre architect Frank Matcham, who also designed the nearby Grand Theatre and Tower Ballroom interiors. This seated 2,500 patrons, was opened in 1889, and was named Her Majesty's Opera House. This theatre closed in late 1910 for building work. The year

1911 saw the re-opening of the new 3,000-seat Opera House. In 1938, the theatre was demolished and, just a year later, the new Art Deco-style Opera House opened its doors to the public.

The early 1930s saw the opening of the Spanish Hall (designed in the style of an Andalusian village), the period-style Renaissance Room, and the Baronial Hall (which resembles the interior of a medieval castle). Other great experiences have sadly been and gone, including the gigantic Ferris wheel, which opened within the complex in 1896 and entertained visitors until its closure in 1928, and removal soon after.

There have been numerous sightings of ghosts and reports of paranormal activity within the complex.

The Opera House

There are several areas within the Opera House where unexplained phenomena has taken place, none more so than the theatre's vast auditorium.

The exterior of the famous Blackpool Winter Gardens as it looked in 1880. (Photo courtesy of Local and Family History Centre, Blackpool Central Library)

The Blackpool Winter Gardens foyer.
(Photo by Stephen Mercer)

The Floral Hall, leading to the Pavilion
Theatre. (Photo by Stephen Mercer)

Uniformed Visitors

John and his girlfriend Ann decided to leave their stalls seats and go to the bar during the interval of a show at the Opera House. They were walking towards the back of the auditorium, where there were fewer people, so they could make their way across to the exits to get drinks. As they reached the back of the auditorium, John thought it was strange to see a man dressed in a uniform pass them by. He watched as the man walked along the back of the seating area, then turned and strolled down the centre aisle.

John watched as the man disappeared into a crowd of other theatregoers. The strange thing was, he didn't reappear. John looked at the seats around the group of people; there was no one there in a uniform. John couldn't place the uniform but later, when he was describing what he had seen to Ann, she thought his description was that of an RAF uniform.

There have been other reports of men in uniform seen in the stalls area. Gemma was on a ghost tour of the theatre and, while standing on the stage, she took some photographs of the auditorium. While showing her friend Julie some of the images on her camera, she noticed that there were a few extremely bright orbs grouped together in one area. They both decided to investigate further.

On their way to the seats, Gemma stopped abruptly and gasped. She could see

Paranormal investigators explore the stage and auditorium of the impressive Opera House. (Photo by Stephen Mercer)

around twenty figures sitting together, and they all looked like they were wearing uniforms; some were wearing hats. She turned to Julie and pointed. Julie looked but could not see anything. When Gemma looked again the figures had gone. She sat down in a seat, and as she did so she felt a breeze pass by her. She was sure that someone from the spirit world had just walked past.

It is said that electrical equipment can drain of power when the presence of a spirit being is near. Paranormal investigator Peter experienced this first hand. He was on a ghost hunt in the Opera House, using his camera to take photographs of the different areas that he and the others in the group were visiting. On entering the stalls, his camera was working perfectly; however, in one small area it would not function – the same area where a group of spectral RAF airmen have been seen.

It is no surprise that people have seen men in uniform in the Opera House; during the Second World War, the town was a major RAF training centre.

The Joker

Above the stage, on the fly floor, it has been reported that the ghost of a gentleman will occasionally make himself known to those working in area. Some staff members call him 'The Joker' as he is a mischievous soul and sometimes plays pranks on people. He occasionally moves objects around, such as the ropes that are attached to the bars that hold the scenery, and he has been known to nudge people when they are waiting on a cue to fly in scenery or props.

A Ghostly Performance for the Cast of *Riverdance*

One of the most popular theatrical spectaculars in the world is the phenomenon that is *Riverdance*. On one occassion when the hit show was touring the UK, it played at the Opera House. Some of the cast had heard stories from members of the theatre staff that the theatre was haunted. They wanted to experience the phantoms of the Opera House for themselves, and asked to be taken on a late-night ghost hunt.

Around thirty members of the company gathered together after one of their breathtaking performances, excited about the possibility of experiencing something from the beyond. For the majority of them, this was a new experience – it would also be a night they would never forget.

They were given equipment to use on their ghost hunt: EMF meters, dowsing rods, pendulums, and thermometers. After explaining how they could use the equipment, the lights were turned off. It was decided that they would visit four areas: the stalls, circle, under the stage and the fly floor. The intrepid ghost hunters were led to the stalls, where they began their evening of investigation and experiments.

One member of the group was using a set of dowsing rods. She held them out in front of her and the rods began to move from side to side. After a moment or two, the rods settled and pointed in the direction of the centre aisle. She decided to walk in whatever direction the rods pointed until they crossed each other. After walking along in front of the stage to the aisle, the rods pointed towards the back of the auditorium; she continued to walk in that direction.

The cast of the hit show Riverdance take a break from performing to experience a ghost tour of the Opera House. (Photo by Stephen Mercer)

The remaining members of the cast and company of Riverdance visit the fly floor in search of 'The Joker'. (Photo by Stephen Mercer)

The rods finally crossed just a few feet from the back of the auditorium. She stopped walking and sat down in one of the seats beside the aisle. She remained seated for a few minutes and then stood, ready to move on to a different area. As she began to walk further along the aisle, she felt pressure in the centre of her back and then she was pushed forwards. She quickly looked behind her, but she was on her own; the rest of the group were spread out in different areas. She hurried away to join other members of the company; she didn't want to be on her own any more!

Three of the company were sitting on the stage looking out into the auditorium. They all heard a noise, which seemed to come from directly behind them. The three moved onto the stage and went in search of whatever had made the sound. They quickly searched the entire area, thinking it could have been another member of the company playing tricks on them, but when they regrouped they realised that nobody else was on the stage but them. Whoever – or whatever – had made the sound had simply vanished.

The group moved on to the circle. Some of the group were beneath the seating in the public walkway, where theatregoers could sit and enjoy a quiet drink in one of the many alcoves there. Whilst sitting at a table in one of the alcoves, a door in front of them opened and closed by itself. Together, they went to the door to see what could make it open and close with no one near it. They looked around the area and realised that they were on their own and there were no draughts that could make the door open and close as it had before. Who was the unseen prankster?

When the group had gathered together back on the stage, they were then ushered down some stairs, to directly beneath the stage.

It was here that some of the company tried using dowsing rods and pendulums. The rods kept pointing to one area – next to the stairs that, if climbed, would take them to the stage again. Some of the group stood next to the bottom step and began to ask questions, to see if any ghost or spirit beings would reply. They heard footsteps coming from above them. One of the group ran back up the stairs and onto the stage to ensure that there was nobody above them responsible for the sound of the footsteps. When he returned a few minutes later, he was able to confirm to everyone that the stage was indeed empty.

They called out again, hoping they would hear the same noise; and indeed they did. The sound of footsteps carried on for around two or three minutes. Again the stage was checked and again was found to be empty. Some of the cast and company were so spooked that they decided to leave. What had made the sound of footsteps – was it a ghostly presence trying to make itself known?

The final area some visited was the fly floor. They had been told about the ghost fondly known by the staff as 'The Joker' and wanted to go in search of him. They climbed the stairs and walked across the bridge to the far side of the fly floor. Those who had pendulums started to ask questions to see if there was a presence nearby. One of the ladies got a response; her pendulum began moving forwards and backwards. When she asked if the presence was the ghost that some of the theatre staff called The Joker, the pendulum started to swing in a circular motion, spinning faster and faster. Another in the group asked if he would make something move, and within seconds the pendulum was pulled away from the lady and shot a few feet across the floor. The group decided to end the ghost hunt at that point and return to the safety of the stage!

Spotlight on Fred the Ghost

At the back of the theatre's auditorium is the spotlight room, also known as the projector room. Footsteps have been heard in the room, as if someone is pacing back and forth. It is believed to be the spirit of Fred, who was a spotlight operator at the theatre many years ago. If the room is not tidy and kept to his liking, he is known to move things around. Staff have also heard the sound of whistling from inside the empty room if they go near it.

Drinks for Two

Beneath the seating, in the circle, is a public area where patrons of the theatre can sit and enjoy a drink in one of the alcoves. A gentleman and lady have been seen to walk through the open doorway and sit down in one of the alcoves. Straight away,

A group of ghost hunters try to contact the couple who sit in the alcove. (Photo by Peter Taylor)

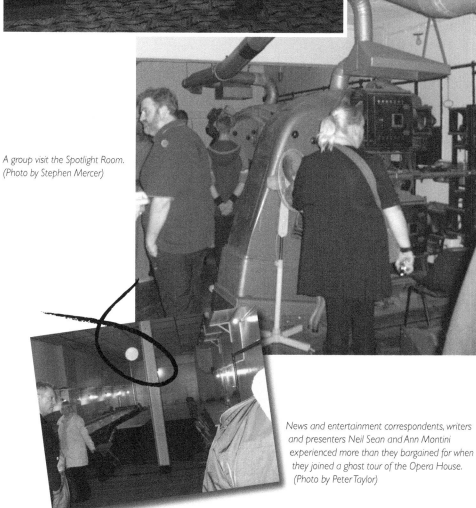

A group visit the Spotlight Room. (Photo by Stephen Mercer)

News and entertainment correspondents, writers and presenters Neil Sean and Ann Montini experienced more than they bargained for when they joined a ghost tour of the Opera House. (Photo by Peter Taylor)

the gentleman stands and walks back out, while the lady stays seated. Almost immediately, he is seen returning to the seat carrying two cocktail glasses, which he sets down on the table in front of them. The couple lift their glasses and toast each other, then, at the sound of the two glasses clinking each other, the couple fade away.

Under-Stage Antics

One of the spookiest areas of the Opera House is under the stage. There have been reports of lights switching on and off on their own, and the shadow of a figure wandering from directly beneath the stage into a room nearby.

NBC reporter and former Sky News entertainment correspondent Neil Sean was taking part in an overnight investigation along with writer, presenter and newspaper columnist Ann Montini. Both Neil and Ann share a love of old theatres and were fascinated by some of the areas normally out of bounds to members of the public.

Towards the end of the night's investigation, they were led by their tour guide beneath the stage. One of the areas they visited was 'wardrobe' – a large room that by day feels light and airy, but by night is cold and gloomy. Neil was persuaded to enter the room first. Hesitantly, he walked through the doorway. It was very dark and only a small amount of light from the corridor behind him shone into the room. As he walked further inside, Neil realised they were not alone.

He could see the silhouette of someone walking away towards the far corner of the room. Ann was behind him, followed by their tour guide. When Neil told the others that he thought there was someone else in the room, the guide asked out loud if anyone was there. The figure stopped for a brief second, then seemed to disappear into the darkness of the room. The guide switched on his torch and pointed it in the direction of where Neil had seen the figure. There was no one there...

The Spanish Hall

The Spanish Hall, with its small stage at one end, a dressing room on either side, a beautiful parquet floor that rivals many ballrooms, and balconies containing three-dimensional representations of Spanish villages, is as unique as it is beautiful.

Spooky sounds, including footsteps, bells ringing and whispering voices, have been heard but not attributed to anyone or anything living!

Phantom Footsteps

Phil, who works at the Winter Gardens, had a scary experience one night while locking up the Spanish Hall. He had locked all the doors leading into the hall except one, which would take him back to the main foyer area. As he was walking across the hall, he heard footsteps behind him. He looked around but there was no one there. He carried on walking, a little faster this time. Reaching the final door out of the hall, he quickly left and locked the door behind him.

He asked a colleague to return with him to the Spanish Hall to check that he

The beautiful Andalusian-inspired interior of the Spanish Hall. (Photo by Sean Conboy, Photo-Genics)

Paranormal investigators discussing what they experienced on a ghost tour in the haunted Spanish Hall. (Photo by Stephen Mercer)

had not locked anyone in the room. They searched the hall and all the rooms leading off it, but no one was found. So to whom did the footsteps belong?

Gail was on an overnight ghost investigation in the Spanish Hall. She was investigating a long staircase that led down to a now unused external door. Earlier in the evening, other members of the group had experienced cold spots and heard whispering noises, and Gail decided to explore the area for herself.

She walked down the flight of stairs to the bottom and, after a few minutes, decided to climb them again and re-join the rest of the group. She was around the halfway mark when she thought she heard footsteps behind her. She stopped for a moment, thinking the sound might have been an echo from her own footsteps, and then she carried on. After a few seconds, she heard the steps again. They still sounded like they were coming from behind her, a little further down the stairs. But she knew that couldn't be right as she had been to the bottom and she had been on her own.

Nervously, she started to ascend the stairs with a little more speed. When the footsteps started to get closer to her, she ran up the rest of the steps to the top landing. Before she opened the door to join the others in the main hall, she looked back. There was no one to be seen.

Actresses and Clowns

Psychic medium and exorcist Ian Lawman spent the night investigating the reported activity that has taken place in the Spanish Hall. During the evening, he experienced much paranormal activity. He saw the shade of a lady walk across the floor of the hall and down a flight of stairs. When he went down the stairs to the door at the bottom, she had gone. Ian sensed that she was an actress and spent time in one of the dressing rooms. He took some of those who were with him into the dressing room and they took turns at scrying in the large mirror. Two of those who tried this saw a lady staring back at them.

Ian also experienced an emotional vision of a death in the Spanish Hall during his investigation. He saw a man – who was carrying out maintenance work on the lighting rig – fall. He hung on to one of the cloud decorations around the balconies while someone ran to get help, but sadly he lost his grip and fell. Ian found out later from a local historian that a maintenance man had died whilst working in the room.

Tracey, a member of the Winter Gardens staff, was shocked at what stared back at her from a mirror. She was sitting in front of it, concentrating on her reflection. After a short time, her face disappeared; she could still see the rest of her body in the mirror, along with the outline of her shoulders, neck and head, but there were no facial features. Then the image of a clown's face appeared where her own should have been. It wasn't long before she retreated from the dressing room!

Don't Go Down the Stairs!

Clare and her husband Anthony also investigated the Spanish Hall on several occasions. Each time, Clare made her way down a flight of steps leading to an external door, and sensed the same thing – that someone was rushing past her. On one occasion, Clare had a vision of a woman lying on the floor at the foot of the stairs. Steve, a medium, who attended the second investigation with Clare and Anthony, agreed. He too felt that there was someone on the stairway and that there was a female who fell to the bottom of the stairs many years ago.

Stuart and Gareth set up a night vision camera at the top of the stairs, pointing downwards. When they checked the footage they discovered many light anomalies, which appeared to be travelling in both directions in the stairwell, and, bizarrely, they also heard dragging and scraping noises. No reason could be found for these scary sounds as no one else was present.

Doors Opening... and Closing on Their Own!

The doors to the gents' toilets have been known to open and close on their own.

The staircase leading down to an exit where Clare felt an unseen spirit brush past her. (Photo by Stephen Mercer)

Peter was with a group of people who were asked to investigate the area. Whilst he and the others were inside the toilet, the door opened and shut. Sisters Jenna and Jane witnessed this unexplainable event.

Roger was on a ghost hunt when he witnessed the door opening and closing. On all of these occasions there was no one near the door, there were no draughts, and there was no logical explanation for the door to open and close on its own. Was someone from the spirit world playing tricks on them?

The Pavilion Theatre

The Pavilion Theatre is situated in the centre of the Horseshoe, which was originally used as a promenade space during the early years of the Winter Gardens complex. It was built as a glass-domed winter garden, hence the name of the complex. It was converted into a theatre 'proper' in the late 1880s, and during the 1930s became a cinema, showing the popular talkies of the era. Sadly, after the cinema closed, it was little used until it was refurbished in the 1990s.

The Lady of the Pavilion

The figure of an elderly lady has often been seen wandering in and around the theatre and the Horseshoe area. She has been seen towards the back of the stage and even in one of the theatre's boxes.

An unusual incident involved Steve, a medium who was attending a ghost investigation at the theatre. There are two boxes on either side of the stage; in the top box, to the right of the stage, he could see the face of a lady looking down at him. He asked a member of the Winter Gardens staff who was accompanying the group if there was anyone up there. He was told that the public were not allowed to go into the boxes because of renovation work that was being carried out there and on the balcony level.

One of the staff members took Steve up to the box to show him that no one from the theatre or the ghost-hunting group was there. Photographs were taken of the box from floor level while they were making their way to it, and, in one image, a single bright orb could be seen in the box. When Steve appeared in the box, more photographs were taken; when these photographs were checked, there was again a single bright orb, but this time it was situated just outside. Another photograph taken after the medium had left the box shows the orb back inside the box. Could this light anomaly be the lady in question? Happy to be in the box by herself but moving aside when the medium entered?

Dressing Room Reflections

Winter Gardens staff member Tracey spent time backstage in the Pavilion, an area that is not open to the public. A few dressing rooms still remain, and as she walked into one of them, she could see the face of a clown in a mirror in front of her. Was this the same clown that she and others have seen in the Spanish Hall?

Two photographs taken within seconds of each other of the box in the Pavilion Theatre. (Photos by Stephen Mercer)

Knock, Knock – Who's There?

Strange noises have been heard by people inside the theatre, which seem to come from the vicinity of the Horseshoe. On one such occasion, James and Darren heard loud knocking sounds and, realising they were coming from outside the theatre, went into the surrounding Horseshoe promenade area to investigate. The noises were extremely loud. They followed the sound of the knocking until they reached the top of some steps. The knocking stopped. They descended and reached a glass door at the bottom, which was locked. As they stood in front of the door, the knocking started again. It was coming from directly in front of them, from the door itself. They could see the door moving slightly, but not enough to cause such loud noises. They could see through the glass in the door, but there was no one on the other side of it. Both James and Darren decided at that point to leave!

Empress Ballroom

The Empress Ballroom was built in 1896 and was one of the largest in the world, with 12,500 square feet of flooring. It is a beautiful room with ornate chandeliers hanging throughout the barrel-vaulted ceiling. Its decorative balconies hold two upper viewing floors, ideal for watching the dancers on its parquet flooring.

The dressing room mirror, where Tracey saw the reflection of a clown's face. If you look closely at this photograph, you may see him too. (Photo by Scott Hatchell)

The ornate balconies in the Winter Gardens' Empress Ballroom. (Photo by Stephen Mercer)

During the First World War, much of the Winter Gardens complex was used by naval and military forces. The ballroom was requisitioned by the Admiralty in 1918 to assemble gas envelopes for the R.33 airship. It was given back a year later and work began to restore the ballroom. Twelve months later, the beautiful room was open for business and hosted the first Blackpool Dance Championships, as it has done every year since, with the exception of a five-year period during the Second World War.

Towards the end of 1934, the Empress Ballroom was re-floored, with 10,000 pieces of oak, mahogany, walnut and greenwood, laid over 1,320 4-inch springs. It is one of the few purpose-built sprung-floor ballrooms in existence today.

The Empress Ballroom has become one of the most diverse venues within the Winter Gardens complex. Pop and rock concerts, political conferences, International Hairdressing Championships and the World Matchplay Darts Tournament have all taken place in this great room, as well as numerous dance festivals and competitions.

Flashing Lights

A group enjoying a ghost tour of the ballroom were split into two smaller groups. Each was accompanied by a member of staff while they were moved to different areas; one group went onto the first-floor balcony level, whilst the other stayed at

The Empress Ballroom. (Photo by Stephen Mercer)

The step from the Empress Ballroom dance floor to the walkway, where the ghost of a young boy has been seen. (Photo by Stephen Mercer)

floor level. It was dark in the ballroom; all the lighting had been switched off. Some were discussing experiences that had taken place earlier that evening; some were sitting quietly, watching.

Suddenly, the chandeliers started to flash on and off, not in unison, but at different times, all independent of each other. The staff on duty that evening could not explain why or how this could happen. When the lights are switched on or off from the main lighting control panel, they can only be switched on together.

The Lost Boy

The apparition of a young boy has been seen in the Empress Ballroom, sitting on a step to one side of the dance floor. He has been described as looking lost, and is all alone. Some have begun to walk around the dance floor to ask if he is okay, but on getting close to where he sits they find he has already gone.

Claire and Mark were at the bar when they saw the young boy. They watched him for a few moments; they were both a little worried as he sat with his head in his hands, looking miserable. After a short time, Claire decided that she should go and ask him if he was okay; no one else had even acknowledged him. She thought it strange that his parents would let him just sit there on his own.

She started walking towards him, weaving in and out of the people on the dance floor. The boy didn't move. He looked so sad. Claire walked around a group of people; when she had got past – he had gone. When she returned to Mark, he asked why she hadn't talked to the boy. Claire explained that when she had reached the step where the boy was sitting, he had already gone. She thought his parents or those who were with him must have called him away or collected him as she walked around the group of people on the dance floor.

Mark was surprised and a little concerned. He told her that she had stopped right next to the boy. Mark had seen her looking around, but what he had noticed more was that the boy had lifted his head and looked up at Claire, smiled, stood up and then disappeared!

Lee and his family were participating in a ghost investigation in the Empress Ballroom. Lee uses audio and video recording equipment when investigating, in the hope that he might be able to capture and document indisputable paranormal evidence.

He set up digital audio recording equipment on a section of the walkway going around the main dance floor, hoping to capture some EVP (electronic voice phenomenon). He moved some distance away to ensure that if any noises or voices were captured by the recorder, it could not be attributed to him.

When he was reviewing his findings from the investigation just days later, he discovered that one extremely shocking piece of audio had been recorded next to the dance floor – the shrill scream of a young child. Was this the scream of the boy who has been seen in that area?

The Creaking Staircase

Radio presenter Mark Howard of Preston FM was taking part in a ghost investigation of the Empress Ballroom on Halloween night. He was part of a small group sitting in the first balcony area. They decided to call out, hoping they would get a response from any ghosts that had decided to pay them a visit. Within seconds, they heard the sound of creaking stairs.

Another member of the group tried to communicate with the ghost, asking the spirit to make the same noises again. Almost immediately, they heard the creaking sounds again. They also heard tapping noises, whispering voices and felt cold spots in the same area. Who was trying to contact Mark and the others in his group?

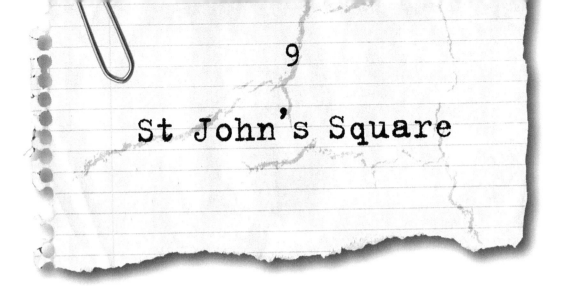

9

St John's Square

DIRECTLY adjacent to the Winter Garden's Church Street entrance is St John's Square, home to Blackpool's first church, the Church of St John the Evangelist, which was consecrated in 1821. The Square also hosts The Wave sculpture, with modern pebbles around its base and illuminated dancing water flumes.

During good weather, you can often see children playing around the water flumes, running in and out, and trying to make it from one side to the other without getting wet; however, what one wouldn't expect to see are the ghosts of a young boy and girl playing there as the sun goes down in the evening.

The Spirits of the Water Fountains

Jane recollects walking through St John's Square at the end of a busy workday on her way home. She could hear children's laughter coming from the fountains and looked up to see two young children playing. Jane smiled as the children squealed with delight as the water flumes shot high into the air, soaking them as they tried to run through and between them. She realised that they were on their own – there were no adults with them – and she thought that very unusual. She had seen this sight many times – children playing in the fountains – but there were always adults close by, usually sitting on the wall beside the fountains, watching over them.

She decided to ask the children – who looked around the ages of 11 or 12 – who was looking after them, and began to walk towards them – but, as she got closer, they ran into the fountain and disappeared. Jane stopped abruptly, trying to figure out what had happened. She tried to make herself believe they had simply run through the fountains and out the other side, towards the main street, but she could see down the street; there were no children in sight.

Aaron and Lucy had been for a meal after work. They were walking through St John's Square towards a taxi rank, so they could get a cab to take them home. They were passing by the fountains when Lucy saw two young children, a boy and a girl,

The water flumes in St John's Square, with the Winter Gardens and Blackpool Tower in the background. (Photo by Sean Conboy, Photo-Genics)

walking towards them. Aaron and Lucy continued across the Square; they could see the taxis queued up at the rank on the other side. As they neared the end of the Square, Lucy looked back over her shoulder; she was wondering where the boy and girl had gone. She turned around and could see that the children were at the fountains. They were taking it in turns to run through the jets of water, laughing at each other as they got wet.

Lucy stopped and watched for a moment; seeing the children enjoying themselves made her laugh out loud, which made Aaron stop walking and turn to her. She nodded towards the fountains, saying she was laughing at the two children playing in them. Aaron looked at her and accused her of having had too much wine with her dinner – there were no children!

Who are the little boy and girl? Could they be the spirits of two children who were buried in the graveyard which, many years ago, was attached to St John's Church?

The children have been seen in other areas of St John's Square too. In the pedestrianised area, next to cafés and shops, there is a wishing well. Many people passing by will stop and throw in a coin or two, making a secret wish. The children have

The wishing well in the foreground and the Secret Garden behind (the white building to the left), where the spirits of a boy and girl play. (Photo by Stephen Mercer)

been seen playing tag, chasing each other around the well.

Debbie and her friends were celebrating a successful day shopping with a glass of wine outside a restaurant. Next to them was the large wishing well. Debbie could hear the water running into the well and noticed two children playing around the well. She watched as they played a game of tag; the boy would chase the girl, and when he caught her he tapped her on the shoulder and then they would turn around, running in the opposite direction with the girl chasing the boy. This game of tag continued for a few minutes.

The children were laughing. Debbie smiled as the children enjoyed their game;

they seemed so happy and carefree. She watched as they ran around the well, out of sight for just a second or two, before reappearing as they rushed past her and her friends sitting at the table. After a moment or two, the laughter from the children suddenly stopped as they ran around the far side of the well. The children didn't reappear this time. She thought that they might have been hiding; perhaps they had seen her watching them and were playing a trick on her.

Debbie stood up and walked around the well, but there were no children. She asked her friends if they had seen where the boy and girl had gone. Her friends had not seen any children… had she imagined it? She doesn't think so; she does believe that she saw two ghosts though.

Mark arrived at the pavement café, where he was meeting his wife Christine for coffee. He chose a table outside and sat down, browsing the drinks menu. Out of the corner of his eye he caught sight of two small figures passing by his table; he looked up to see a young boy and girl walking away from him, towards the shop next to the café that he called the 'Fairy Shop' because of the items the shop sold: hanging fairies, crystals, jewellery and angels, amongst many other bits and pieces.

The children stopped in front of the shop's large window and, simultaneously, they placed their hands on the pane of glass and stared inside. He could see their faces light up at the wonderment of the shop's interior. He was not surprised; he had been inside the Secret Garden many times and could understand why children would be so astonished by the scene in front of them. A waitress arrived to take his order; he was

expecting his wife to arrive at any moment so he ordered two coffees and then continued watching the children in front of the shop window.

They were pointing at items in the window display – pieces of jewellery and crystals hanging from a tree; figurines sitting beside a water fountain. Every now and then he could hear them giggling. He was jolted back to reality as his wife sat down opposite him. She asked why he was smiling and staring at a shop window. He laughed and said he was watching the two children, who were staring in amazement at the items in the window's display. Christine interrupted him, saying that there was no one looking in the window. He looked for himself and indeed the children had gone; he said they must have left at the same time that his wife sat down. Christine was a little confused at this, as she had been able to see both her husband and the shop he was staring at as she walked to their table, and at no time had she seen any children looking in its window.

10

The Grand Theatre

THE Grand Theatre was commissioned by theatre manager Thomas Sergenson and designed by renowned architect Frank Matcham, who also designed the interiors of Blackpool Tower Ballroom and the original Opera House. Work was to begin on the building of the Grand Theatre and Opera House, as it was originally to be named, in 1888; however, the owners of the Winter Gardens began to build the Opera House within its complex. Sergenson delayed the construction of the Grand Theatre, and in 1889 opened the Grand Circus on the land instead.

For five summers a different circus was engaged to entertain Blackpool visitors, until Sergenson closed the Grand Circus in 1893 to commence work on the long-awaited Grand Theatre. Less than a year later, on 23 July 1894, the Grand Theatre opened its doors for the first time with a performance of *Hamlet*. Sergenson successfully owned and managed the theatre until 1909, when he sold it to the Blackpool Tower Company, which ran the theatre until 1972 when it applied for permission to demolish the theatre in favour of a department store. The theatre, however, had become a listed building, so a full enquiry was launched. Second World War veteran A. Burt Briggs, barrister John Hodgson, and other theatre fans, rallied together and petitioned against the plan. The Friends of the Grand was formed in 1973 to fight the cause and, later that year, was successful in keeping the Grand Theatre safe from the wrecking ball.

The Grand Theatre was saved; however, it was closed for some years and was utilised as a bingo hall in others. In 1980, the Grand Theatre Trust Ltd was set up and purchased the theatre. The Friends came together and decorated and refurbished dressing rooms and backstage areas in preparation for the reopening of the theatre on 23 March 1981. On 29 May of the same year, the Grand Theatre had the honour of hosting a Royal Variety Performance in the presence of HRH the Prince of Wales. The theatre has continued to be successful to this day, presenting some of the most popular touring productions in the country.

But, what goes on behind the scenes at the Grand? What ghosts have been seen

The exterior of the Grade II* listed Grand Theatre. (Photo by Stephen Mercer)

The Grand Theatre – Victorian design and architecture at its best. (Photo by Sean Conboy, Photo-Genics)

and what strange supernatural activity has occurred? There have been numerous reports of ghostly sightings within the theatre, including a man (who has been nicknamed Charlie by theatre staff), wandering in the upper circle level, and a woman who has been seen beneath the stage. The sound of footsteps have been heard coming from above those who stand on the stage; light anomalies, believed by many to be orbs, have been captured in both photograph and video form in the auditorium; and cold spots have been felt by many who have investigated this beautiful Victorian theatre! It seems to many who investigate the strange goings-on in the Grand Theatre that it is the haunted hotspot of Blackpool!

Charlie

Charlie's tale is a sad story of unrequited love. He is said to have visited the theatre during the 1930s and, whilst watching a play, he became infatuated with its leading lady and fell head over heels in love with her. He would sit in the same seat in the front row of the upper circle night after night, performance after performance. Before each show, he would regularly wait at the stage door just to catch a glimpse of her. He would leave her gifts and send her flowers; but his presents to her were always returned. After attending the theatre night after night and having his advances spurned, he took the ultimate revenge and hurled himself to his death from the upper circle balcony level, in a final dramatic bid for her attention.

It is said that he can be seen sitting in the front row of the upper circle seating, notice-able because of his out-of-place clothing. He has also been spotted at the back of the seating area close to the entrance of the bar, which was once known as the Gentleman's Bar.

Regular theatre tours are run at the Grand, where members of the public are given an opportunity to see inside the beautiful auditorium, stand on the stage, visit back and under-stage areas, and take a peek inside the dressing rooms – and hear a ghost story or two!

Grand staff member David Fletcher regularly leads the daytime heritage tours of the theatre. One of the spooky stories he tells on his tours took place in 1999. The Drifters were performing one evening to an enthusiastic crowd. A girlfriend of one of the band members made herself known to one of the theatre's ushers in the stalls during the interval, and asked if the theatre had any ghosts. The usher replied that there were stories of a ghost that roamed one or two areas in the theatre. The lady pointed to the second balcony level, to the doorway of the bar, and asked if that was where the ghost had been seen because during the show she had seen a man standing in front of the doorway with a lady on both arms and, from the way they were dressed, they were definitely not members of the audience; they were wearing clothing from the Victorian era. The usher confirmed that that was one of the areas where the ghost had often been seen!

Jan and her husband Eamonn were taking part in one of these tours, listening with interest to the fascinating history that was offered by their tour guide. They had reached the upper circle level and were being taken into the bar, where they would

The upper circle, where the ghost of Charlie may appear. (Photo by Peter Taylor)

see some of the theatre's archived posters and photographs that adorn its walls. As they were about to enter the doors, Eamonn thought he could hear the soft footsteps of someone walking behind them. He thought they were the final two in the party to reach the door, so he was a little surprised.

He turned around and saw that a gentleman was walking towards them. Eamonn remembers that the man was wearing a dark suit with a waistcoat and a hat. He thought that perhaps there was another member of staff on the tour dressed in Victorian period clothing, as their guide was. The man turned and began to walk down the steps of the seating bank, and sat down in the front row.

Jan was by now quite anxious to get into the bar so they didn't miss out on viewing the posters and photographs; she nudged her husband to make him hurry. He apologised and pointed to where the man was sat to explain; the man wasn't there. Eamonn had only taken his eyes off the man in the front row for a few seconds; there was no way he could have walked up the steps and passed them without him seeing or hearing him. Eamonn believes he saw a ghost that day. He was even more surprised when his tour guide told the tale of the theatre's resident ghost, Charlie, who is often seen in the area.

Gail was on a ghost investigation at the Grand Theatre. She had never been on any kind of paranormal event before and was excited at what might happen. Gail had no prior knowledge of any paranormal activities that had been reported as taking place in the theatre, and was pleased that no information had been given to anyone attending the investigation beforehand. She had brought a friend for support, but before long she was off investigating areas for herself. She was part of a smaller group who were taken to the upper circle level.

She decided to sit in a seat next to the aisle in the front row, so she could look down into the stalls area below and onto the stage. She was taking photographs, hoping that she might capture orbs or mists and shadows, when she heard footsteps coming down the steps next to her. It was dark inside the theatre; all the lights had been turned off when they began the investigation earlier that evening. She could make out the figure of a man getting closer to her. She smiled and said hello but the man didn't say anything in return. He simply sat down in the seat opposite her in the front row. Gail thought that perhaps he was so engrossed in what he was doing that he hadn't heard her greet him, so she decided to carry on taking photographs. After just a moment, she decided to move on to another area. She stood up and saw the man stand at the same time. She smiled again and began to say hello to him, but her words wouldn't come out; the man faded in front of her.

Whilst investigating the Grand Theatre for their television programme *Spook School*, paranormal investigative team Para-Projects visited the upper circle level. They were trying to find some logical reasons for some of the reported supernatural activities there. One of the team, Jebby, was sitting in the seat that is believed to be the one where Charlie had sat many years before (and perhaps still does). Jebby was trying to answer a call on a walkie-talkie from Mark and Rob, who were on the stage; however, every time he tried to say anything into the walkie-talkie it would buzz very loudly. There was some interference taking place. Jebby moved around a little to see if he could get a better signal. He moved one seat in either direction; there was no interference. It was only when he sat in 'Charlie's seat' that the buzzing noise could be heard. He also had an EMF meter, a piece of equipment that many ghost hunters use to measure electromagnetic fields as it is believed that ghosts are made up of energy. While he was sat in the seat it would register some form of energy, but when he moved to a seat on either side, the noise ceased and the meter stopped registering energy! Was the interference being caused by Charlie? Was it is his spiritual energy that was being registered on the meter?

The Spooky Seat

A producer who previously brought shows to the Grand would often sit in a seat in the upper circle, watching rehearsals. He was doing just that one late afternoon, writing notes about the performance such as what changes he would like to make. Suddenly, he felt a tap on his shoulder and heard a whisper in his ear. He thought it was someone from the marketing office, which is situated in the upper circle level, playing tricks on him. He rose from his seat and looked around; there was no one there.

Ghost hunters investigate the Grand Theatre stage. (Photo by Stephen Mercer)

He went to the marketing office door, believing that whoever it was who tapped him may have run back to the office; however, the door was locked, there was obviously no one in the office. He returned to his seat. Within a few minutes, he felt the tap again on his shoulder and a cold breeze blowing on the back of his neck and head. He immediately stood up and looked behind the seat. Again, there was no one there or nearby. By this time he was beginning to feel a bit uneasy. He decided to sit one last time and was ready to jump up if he felt anything. He didn't have long to wait. He again felt the cold breeze and heard whispering in his ear. He stood up quickly, spun around, but again he was on his own. He left the area with much haste and decided not to return. He told one of the members of staff what had happened, who told him it was probably the ghost of Charlie playing tricks on him!

On a ghost tour of the Grand Theatre, Steve and several other paranormal enthusiasts were investigating the upper circle area. Steve sat down on a chair to take a moment out and enjoy the atmosphere of the theatre. It was dark and very quiet – not at all what he was used to when he came to see shows at the Grand. He was watching other people further along the row of seats where he was sat when he heard a whispering voice from directly behind him. He turned, expecting to see someone else from the tour, but there was nobody there. He turned around again and immediately heard the whispering voice for a second time. He thought it was perhaps just echoes of the others nearby. He then felt a hand ruffling his hair – he jumped up out of the seat and looked around. No one was there. He thought this very strange but was excited at the possibility that he might be experiencing something paranormal. He sat down again and decided that he would stay there even if his hair was ruffled again.

Within a moment or two he heard the whispering again; this time it sounded like the owner of the voice was stood next to

Psychic medium and exorcist Ian Lawman explains how to use pendulums during a ghost investigation at the Grand Theatre. (Photo by Stephen Mercer)

The Grand Theatre's auditorium.
(Photo by Stephen Mercer)

Suddenly she said out loud that she knew what she had to do.

She walked away from the others who were involved in the experiment and sat down in a seat near the front of the upper circle. She felt that she was not alone and knew that there was the ghost of a little girl with her. She realised that she was to reunite the girl with her father in the spirit world. She sat and talked out loud to the girl and then felt that the father had joined them. It was then that she burst into tears, as she knew father and daughter were together again. Carol still has a tear in her eyes when she remembers that night.

Psychic medium Ian Lawman also saw the father and daughter when he led a ghost walk around the Grand Theatre. He was taking the group of people around the upper circle area to the bar, and telling those with him what he could feel and see. He first felt their presence with him and then saw them stood together nearby, smiling. Ian believes they were happy and used to visit the theatre when they were alive – and now they have passed over, they come back to visit still.

him, with their face just inches away from the side of his. He felt a cold breeze blow along his neck, and once more he felt a hand touch the top of his head. He froze; he couldn't move! He could see there was no one stood next to him but he could feel and sense someone was there. It was too much for him. He yelled and jumped out of his seat, quickly joining other members of the tour. Safety in numbers, he thought!

Father and Daughter Pay a Visit... From the Other Side

Carol and her husband Dave were taking part in an experiment whilst on an overnight vigil at the theatre. They were sitting in the upper circle level and, while conducting the experiment, Carol had the strange feeling that she was supposed to help someone. She couldn't understand what or why and became quite upset. Even now she finds it difficult to describe the sensations she was feeling at the time.

The Lady Under the Stage

Edwina was on her first, and, as she thought at the time, her last, ghost hunt. She experienced something that she believes to be paranormal, something she could not explain then, nor can she explain now! She was with a group of five people in a small room under the stage. The lights had been turned off and the group were stood in a circle, holding hands, calling out to ask if there were any spirits in the room to give them some kind of a sign – to make a noise or to move something within the room that they could all hear or see. They immediately heard tapping noises and two people in the group said they felt that something was standing on their feet. Edwina thought at first it could simply be foot pain or cramp, as they had been standing for quite a long time, but then she became affected in a major way.

Edwina's legs, from the knees down, started to feel like they were on fire, like they were burning. The pain she felt was horrendous and she started shaking. She told the rest of the group but agreed to continue with calling out. The pain got worse and another lady became a little frightened and asked that they stop. Edwina was glad when they all agreed, because at that stage she was unable to move her legs at all. Someone turned the lights on and straight away the pain in Edwina's legs was gone.

Later, when the group were talking about their experiences, Edwina was told that she had stood directly beneath a trap door that had not been used in the theatre for a very long time. There is a story of a lady who was a seamstress at the theatre many years ago. Walking along the stage and not realising that the trap door was open, she had fallen through, injuring herself badly. She was taken to hospital but sadly died. Edwina believes that the pain she felt in her legs could be likened to that of someone who had a serious fall. Was Edwina feeling the pain felt by the spirit of the seamstress under the stage?

Peeking into the room under the stage, where people have experienced what they believe to be paranormal phenomena. (Photo by Peter Taylor)

Peter was on a tour of the Grand and was in the small room under the stage with two other people. At the time, the room was home to a large drum kit belonging to a member of a band that was performing with a show that week in the theatre. The lights were on; the room looked bright and colourful; nothing strange at all. Until they were leaving that is! As the three filed back out the door and it was closing behind them, they heard the clashing sound of one of the cymbals on the kit. They went back in to see what had happened. There was no one else in the room and none of the three could explain why the sound was heard; was it the lady under the stage trying to frighten them?

Johanna was on the stage and decided to venture down under to see the photographs of the theatre that she had been told were hung on the walls. As she was going down the stairs, she saw the shadow of a figure passing the bottom step along the corridor beneath the stage. She thought it was a member of staff or someone else on the tour. When she reached the corridor, she looked all around, and called out to see who was there. She realised there was nobody else with her under the stage. She didn't stay there for long; in fact, she never even got to see the photographs!

John was with a group of people who were taking a tour of the theatre. Their guide had brought them under the stage, an area where the general public would never get to see. They were about to be led up the stairs onto the stage itself. John was at the end of the group of visitors and, just as he was about to ascend the stairs, he heard one of the doors opening and then closing. He stopped climbing, as did the two ladies who were in front of him; they had heard the noise too. They knew there was no one else under the stage, as they had all looked in the rooms and they were the only people there. John had heard stories of a ghostly presence that had been seen under the stage by people on ghost tours. He told the two ladies and together they decided to go look for themselves. They walked back down the corridor, opening each door in turn and looking in each room. Nobody was there; each room was empty! They hurried back to join the rest of the tour group on the stage.

Rob from Para-Projects decided to investigate under the stage; he wishes now that he had let another member of the team do it! He volunteered to sit in a room on his own while everyone else remained outside. Rob has investigated many reported haunted locations and has been locked in rooms on his own before; he thought he would be fine. Rob managed to stay in the room for just a few minutes.

Whilst in the room, he felt that there was another person there. He knew there couldn't be as there was only one door in and out, and he was the last person to use it. He felt a chill around him and then the room became very cold. He didn't like the room at all and decided enough was enough when he heard a noise coming from the corner. He left very quickly. Was it the ghost of the lady trying to get him to leave the room? He believes so.

Footsteps from Above

There are many stories of people who have been on the theatre's stage and have heard footsteps crossing the bridge above it. The bridge is a narrow walkway, approximately 30 feet above the stage that leads to the fly floor – an area where stage crew operate ropes that 'fly' in and out the scenery for shows. When there is a show in progress, or when people are on the stage, no one is allowed, due to health and safety reasons, to cross the bridge to the fly floor. So why, when there have been people on the stage, have footsteps been heard as if someone is crossing the bridge?

Psychic Ian Lawman was conducting a séance on the stage with a group of people on one of his ghost walks of the theatre. He sensed a spirit above the stage, so called out, asking for the being to make a sound. His request was answered with footsteps coming from above them on the bridge. Ian asked for the same noise to occur again; it did.

A member of the theatre's staff was there and Ian asked him to check if anyone was up on the bridge or the fly floor. He took another member of the group with him and they made their way to the door which led to the floor. Ian carried on asking for the noises to continue, and each time the footsteps could be heard. They only stopped when the two who went to investigate the floor area arrived and shouted down to those on the stage that there was no one else there!

Grand Theatre staff member David Fletcher tells the story of how a security guard was stopped in his tracks as he crossed the bridge by an unseen entity. During a time of closure, security guards would come into the theatre to ensure that everything was as it should be; doors closed, windows locked, etc.

Late one evening, two guards were doing their rounds of the building. They climbed

Walking across the bridge to the fly floor, 30 feet above the stage! (Photo by Stephen Mercer)

the stairs backstage which led to dressing rooms, checking that all the rooms were secure, and then made their way through the door that leads to the bridge to cross over to the fly floor. Les, one of the security guards, was the first to step onto the bridge. He managed to walk half its distance when he was forced to stop. He felt like he was being held in place by someone, or something, that he couldn't see. Whatever that unseen force was, it would not let him take another step forward no matter how hard he tried. Les felt nervous and frightened; he called out to the other security guard and slowly made his way back to join his colleague. They swiftly completed their rounds of the theatre and returned to their supervisor's office, which was situated at the Winter Gardens.

Les told his supervisor what had happened. His supervisor told him not to worry as it was probably just Charlie doing his late-night rounds too. He said there was no need to be nervous as Charlie wouldn't

A view of the bridge leading to the fly floor, taken from the stage. What stopped the security guard from walking across? Was it Charlie? (Photo by Stephen Mercer).

From left to right: Angus Purden, Danniella Westbrook, Derek Acorah, Stephen Mercer.

hurt anyone; he just likes to make himself known to people every now and again.

Derek Acorah's Ghost Towns

Spirit medium Derek Acorah brought his paranormal investigative television series *Derek Acorah's Ghost Towns* to Blackpool in 2005 and one of the locations visited was the Grand Theatre. Not long after arriving, Derek was standing on the stage with his co-hosts Danniella Westbrook and Angus Purden, some of his film crew and three theatre staff members. The filming had begun and Derek was talking about what he was feeling around him on the stage when he was interrupted by sounds that came from above them.

Above them was the bridge; the walkway that leads to the fly floor. The sounds heard, were described by those on the stage as footsteps. A member of the theatre's staff was sent to investigate whether anyone was on the bridge or the fly floor, however, on his return just a few moments later, it was confirmed there was no one there. What, or who, could have made the noises?

Derek and Danniella visited the bridge shortly afterwards, however, as Derek began to make his way across to the fly floor, he was overcome with emotion and felt a presence close by which would not let him complete his journey and he had to turn back. Was this the same spirit who also stopped the security guard from crossing the walkway many years before?

11

Haunted Hotels & Pubs

Barceló Blackpool Imperial Hotel

Probably the most famous and most historic of the town's hotels is the four-star Barceló Blackpool Imperial Hotel, situated on Blackpool's North Promenade, overlooking the Irish Sea. This fine Victorian hotel was built in 1867 and has been one of the most popular hotels in the town since its opening. In his final years, the novelist Charles Dickens stayed at the hotel, describing it as 'charming'. And charming it most certainly is.

Karen used to work at the Imperial. She has told of how some of the staff who stay there or work on night duties have reported hearing a child crying on a fire escape situated at the back of the hotel. However, when they have gone to check, there is no one there.

When the hotel opened, the basement was originally a livery; the care, feeding and stabling of horses took place here. The sound of horses' hooves has been heard in that area, along with the smell of damp hay.

During the two world wars, the basement was utilised as an infirmary. The basement's usage has changed over the years and now houses the laundry, offices and the hotel's leisure centre. Karen has heard faint moans and the sound of footsteps crossing a stone floor in these areas. When she checked if anyone was there, she found she was alone.

Barceló Blackpool Imperial Hotel. (Photo courtesy of the Imperial Hotel)

The Best Western Carlton Hotel. (Photo courtesy of the Carlton Hotel)

Best Western Carlton Hotel

Another seafront hotel is the Best Western Carlton Hotel. On the ground floor, the hotel has a unique attraction; a well that goes down some depth is situated in one of its restaurants. A favourite with holiday-makers, the hotel is a peaceful and pleasant place... usually.

Shilpa, who runs the hotel, has been told that there are two spirits that occasionally visit the hotel: a lady on the first floor and a gentleman on the ground floor. The lady has been seen roaming one of the corridors on the first floor and disappearing through the wall into one of the bedrooms. Guests staying in that particular room have claimed to have felt someone watching over them. Strange shadows have been viewed in one corner of the room and the lights have been known to turn off and on by themselves.

Next to the restaurant are stairs lead-ing down to toilet facilities. The shadowy figure of a gentleman has been seen walk-ing up and down these stairs. Some believe

the male presence may enter through the well and could be someone who sadly died in one of the ancient shipwrecks that occurred off the coast near the hotel.

The Saddle Inn

Landlady Janet has experienced a number of strange happenings, which she believes to be paranormal, at the Saddle Inn. She has seen objects move along shelves, chairs move in one of the public rooms, and glasses slide along the bar and fall, smashing to the floor. When smoking was permitted in the bar, ashtrays would disappear and then reappear in another room. Perhaps the most terrifying thing for her, though, was the figure of a man in the cellar, who was seen on a number of occasions by herself and another employee.

After an appeal was made in the local Blackpool newspaper, the *Gazette*, a par-anormal investigative team spent an evening at the inn, trying to find out just what was going on. A lot of activity was experienced during the investigation, most of which took place in the cellar. Glasses moved on a shelf and pegs flew from one side of the cellar to the other. A white mist appeared in the corner of the room, and one investigator saw what she believed to be the ghost of a man wearing a flat cap and a long jacket. One of the investigators was monitoring equipment that had been set up in the cellar when a loud scream was heard next to him, causing him to vacate the area with much haste.

Other objects moved of their own accord in the main bar area, including an empty till roll and a spoon, and strange

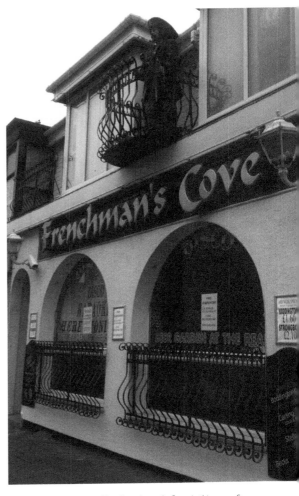

The Saddle Inn. The shadowy figure of a man, not of this realm, has been seen by the landlady in the cellar. (Photo by Stephen Mercer)

The Boars Head: things go bump in the night here – literally! (Photo by Stephen Mercer)

The Frenchman's Cove; is this one of Blackpool's most haunted pubs? The builders certainly thought so! (Photo by Stephen Mercer)

noises were heard throughout the investigation. When the team carried out a séance, three spirit beings made themselves known, one of whom was called Rose, who used to be a cleaner in the pub many years ago. Was it Rose who moved the ashtrays from room to room?

Frenchman's Cove

When the bar and restaurant were being constructed, owner Billy Johnson received many comments from the workmen, who said they felt like someone – or something – was watching them. This mostly took place in the cellar. After hearing this on numerous occasions, the publican decided to go down to see for himself. It was then that Billy realised that his bar had a ghost!

Blackpool Gazette reporter Lisa Ettridge believes that something eerie is going on in the bar. There have been reports that doors open and close in the ladies' toilet – something that she experienced for herself. On a night out, she and a friend visited the Frenchman's Cove for a quiet drink. Before leaving, she visited the ladies' toilet; when she entered, the door closed firmly behind her, however, seconds later, it opened and shut again without anyone else entering the room. She checked behind the door, there was no one there. That was when Lisa decided to leave… quickly.

The Boars Head

Tracy, the landlady at the Boars Head, is convinced that the ghost of a child haunts her pub. Things go missing – often her jewellery – and she is sure that it is a child playing pranks on her. She will put her earrings down in the evening before going to bed and, the next morning, one of the pair will have disappeared. She has also noticed dramatic changes in temperature around the pub, something she attributes to the ghost visiting the premises.

She has regularly heard tapping noises coming from the bar and has also been kept awake at night by banging sounds. One night she was awoken by a racket. The sound of banging was so loud that she got out of bed and went to investigate every room in the pub, from top to bottom. There was nothing to be found, no reason for the noises, but they continued for some time. She finally had enough and went to the top of the stairs and shouted down, telling whoever it was making the noises to stop… they did!

A view of North Pier as the sun begins to set. Blackpool is one of the most beautiful seaside resorts by day, and one of the most haunted by night! (Photo by Juliette W. Gregson, Blackpool Ghosts Photography)

Sources & Web Links

Supernatural Events, founded and run by the author, organises Ghost Tours, Investigations and Blackpool Ghost Walks:

www.SupernaturalEvents.co.uk
www.BlackpoolGhostWalks.com
www.facebook.com/SupernaturalEvents

Barceló Blackpool Imperial Hotel (www.barcelo-hotels.co.uk/blackpool)
Best Western Carlton Hotel (www.bw-carltonhotel.co.uk)
The Blackpool Gazette (www.blackpoolgazette.co.uk)
Blackpool Ghosts (www.blackpoolghosts.co.uk)
Blackpool Ghosts Photography (www.blackpoolghostsphotography.co.uk)
Blackpool North Pier (www.northpierblackpool.co.uk)
Blackpool Parks (www.friendsofstanleypark.org.uk)
Blackpool Tower (www.theblackpooltower.com)
Blackpool Transport (www.blackpooltransport.com)
Blackpool Winter Gardens (www.wintergardensblackpool.co.uk)
Blackpool Zoo (www.blackpoolzoo.org.uk)
Derek Acorah (www.derekacorah.com)
Ian Lawman (www.ianlawman.org)
Local and Family History Centre, Backpool Central Library (www.blackpoolimagegallery.org.uk)
Para-Projects (www.para-projects.com)
Photo-Genics (www.photo-genics.com)
Pleasure Beach Resort (www.blackpoolpleasurebeach.com)
Radio Wave (www.wave965.com)
The Grand Theatre (www.blackpoolgrand.co.uk)
visitBlackpool (www.visitblackpool.com)
Lancashire and Blackpool Tourist Board (www.visitlancashire.com)

Other titles published by The History Press

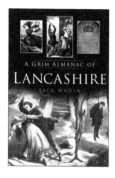

A Grim Almanac of Lancashire
JACK NADIN

A Grim Almanac of Lancashire is a day-by-day catalogue of 365 ghastly tales from around the county, dating from the twelfth to the twentieth centuries. Full of dreadful deeds, macabre deaths, strange occurrences and heinous homicides, this almanac contains diverse tales of highwaymen, murderers, bodysnatchers, poachers, witches, rioters and rebels. All these, plus tales of suicide, explosions, accidents by land, sea and air, and much more, are here.

978 0 7524 5684 3

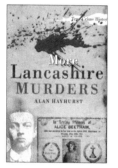

More Lancashire Murders
ALAN HAYHURST

In this chilling follow-up to *Lancashire Murders*, Alan Hayhurst brings together more murderous tales that shocked not only the county but made headline news throughout the nation. These include the case of Oldham nurse Elizabeth Berry, who poisoned her own daughter for the insurance money in 1887; Margaret Walber, who beat her husband to death in Liverpool in 1893; and Norman Green, who was hanged for the murder of two young boys in Wigan in the 1950s.

978 0 7524 5645 4

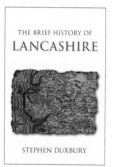

The Brief History of Lancashire
STEPHEN DUXBURY

Racing through the history of Lancashire, with Neolithic residents, Romans, Civil War victories and Victorians – and, of course, a few cotton mills along the way – this delightful book will tell you everything you ought to know about the dramatic and fascinating history of the county – and a few things you never thought you would.

978 0 7524 6288 2

Butlin's: 75 Years of Fun!
SYLVIA ENDACOTT & SHIRLEY LEWIS

From Redcoats to water worlds, and from the Glamorous Grandmothers competitions to National Talent contests, this book provides an enjoyable and nostalgic trip down memory lane for all who know and love Butlin's, allowing the reader a glimpse into the social history of this quintessential British holiday.

978 0 7524 5863 2

Visit our website and discover thousands of other History Press books.
www.thehistorypress.co.uk